Point

of

No Return

A NOVEL BY

ELISSA GABRIELLE

Peace In The Storm Publishing

Praise for Elissa Gabrielle & Point of No Return

"Like her characters, Elissa Gabrielle's writing is hot, sassy, and skillfully witty, giving a whole new meaning to erotica!"
— Jessica Tilles, author of *Unfinished Business*

೧ ೧ ೧

"Few have started with such intriguing and captivating characters who chase, find and sometimes lose love. Her detailed descriptions will undoubtedly put you in a trance, pulling you in deeper. In *Point of No Return*, Gabrielle's brilliance and command is displayed in this romantic, erotic sequel."
— James Lisbon, Founder, *Awareness Magazine*

೧ ೧ ೧

"What happens when forbidden lovers address the aftermath of crossing the Point Of No Return? Elissa Gabrielle answers this intriguing question with a sexy and scintillating sequel to *Good To The Last Drop* that is a definite must read!"
— Bill Holmes, author of *One Love*

"Elissa Gabrielle has penned another great tale in her latest release, *Point of No Return*. She delivers a stunning narrative that is sure to keep you engrossed in the story and hungry for more. Gabrielle draws her reading audience in with a unique tale that is full of humor, sex, scandal and captivating characters. Elissa Gabrielle has proven to be one of the greatest voices in her genre."

— Lalaina Knowles, author of *Twisted Karma*

ও ও ও

"Elissa Gabrielle's writing style is dangerously irresistible and has proven there is spirit in lust and in lust there is a life fighting to love."

— Linda Wattley, author of *Daddy's Girl*

ও ও ও

"Elissa Gabrielle doesn't disappoint with the scorching sequel, Point of No Return. With a fresh writing style, unforgettable characters and a steaming hot storyline; Ms. Gabrielle has effortlessly taken erotica to a whole new level!"

— D.L.Sparks, author of *All That Glitters*

ও ও ও

"Elissa Gabrielle gets her sizzle on in her latest release. With characters who are honest and real enough to tread that thin line between love and hate, she brings you to the brink in *Point of No Return*."

— Janet West Sellars, author of *Quiet As It's Kept*

"*Point of No Return* will take you on a H-O-T and wild ride with characters that are equally wild, sassy and contemporary."
— Vanessa A Johnson, author of *When Death Comes a Knockin*

೩ ೩ ೩

"Elissa Gabrielle is a force to be reckoned with."
— Shani Greene Dowdell, author of *Keepin' it Tight*

೩ ೩ ೩

"Elissa Gabrielle takes HOT to another level in her sizzling novel *Point of No Return*."
— Jahzara, author of *Luv Don't Live Here Anymore*

೩ ೩ ೩

"Elissa Gabrielle is a sexy writing force that deserves more than mere recognition. Her words will take you on a ride of literary pleasure. Gabrielle quenches your erotic thirst and will make you beg for more."
— Wanda D. Hudson, author of *Wait For Love: A Black Girl's Story*

ISBN-13: 978-0-9790222-1-0
ISBN-10: 0-9790222-1-5

This is a work of fiction. All of the characters, incidents, and dialogue, except for incidental references to public figures, products, or services, are imaginary and are not intended to refer to any persons, living or dead, or to disparage any company's products or services. Although the author and publisher have made every effort to ensure the accuracy and completeness of information contained in this book, we assume no responsibility for errors, inaccuracies, omissions, or any inconsistency herein.

ATTENTION CORPORATIONS, UNIVERSITIES, COLLEGES AND PROFESSIONAL ORGANIZATIONS: Quantity discounts are available on bulk purchases of this book for educational, gift purposes, or as premiums for increasing magazine subscriptions or renewals. This is also available to various Book Clubs. Contact the Publisher for more information.

Peace In The Storm Publishing
P.O. Box 1152
Pocono Summit, PA 18346

Visit our Web site at www.PeaceInTheStormPublishing.com

Interior text designed by The Writer's Assistant
www.TheWritersAssistant.com

Also By Elissa Gabrielle

Stand and Be Counted

Peace in the Storm

Good to the Last Drop

"He doesn't know how fucking lucky he is to have you. I try to tell him that all the time, Amber; that he's blessed to have you. So go ahead and say it. No sense in holding anything back, not now... we've already crossed the line, been past the Point of No Return."

—Shawn Fontaine in *Good to the Last Drop*

Point

of

No Return

An Elissa Gabrielle Original

Amber
Revelations

I can't believe it. I simply cannot believe what just happened. As I'm in bed with one of my dearest friends, reflections of what just took place won't leave my head. The event plays over and over again in my mind. I am, without a doubt, frozen in time.

We're both under the sheets, naked. I'm on my back, and Shawn, my husband's best friend, has his head on my breasts. His massive hold of me seems serene. I can feel his heart beating against mine; his breathing is slow.

Shawn seems to be at peace. I wonder if he's thinking what I'm thinking. We've been friends for so long that I hope our friendship is not ruined now. If it's not shot to hell after this episode, I know it's definitely changed. I love my husband dearly, but right now, I'm loving his best friend.

Neither of us have spoken a word since the "*I love you's,*" that poured from our lips in the midst of our adulterated acts of pure ecstasy.

I don't know what to feel, other than confusion. Way too much to consume. The heat. The passion. The groundbreaking lovemaking. The pain. The lies. The betrayal. The tears. The need to make sense of it all, when all of it is really so senseless.

However, I do know, at this moment, that Shawn and I need to face reality. We've been through so much together. I pray we'll get through this. I'm almost afraid to speak. When I finally do summons the courage, my cell phone rings again. It's playing *Big Pimpin'* by Jay Z. My favorite ring tone breaks the silence.

It can only be one person, Khalil. His special ring tone. He's been blowing up my phone since he left for Virginia. I have spoken to him a few times. On the last phone call, I was crying so hard, trying to get the words out. I'm sure; however, he barely understood what I tried to say. I'm sure he managed to hear the words, *bachelor party*, amidst my sobs.

I've forgiven Khalil for his indiscretions so many times before. This time should be no different, but it is. The humiliation was actually in my face. All too real. This time, I was familiar with Khalil's drug of choice. I was afforded the opportunity of, not only knowing his *sexcapades*, but also actually hanging out with one, and seeing the other at my place of employment, from time to time. Of course, I found out about his betrayals many times over in the past, but this time is different.

In the past, I'd never had the pleasure of putting a face to any of the names...except for Shayla. I didn't have to face the reality of knowing who my man was attracted to, who my man would give himself to, who my man would lie to me for, who my man would love in addition to me. Never got to put a face to the betrayal. Until now.

It hurts so badly. And, just to think, I actually knew these two bitches! And Loreatha of all people! Or should I say, *Chyna*? Once she found out Khalil was my husband, nothing but death could've kept her from gloating.

I will never understand why Black women hate each other so much, but we do. Anything to keep the next woman down. Whether it's a mental, emotional, or a physical put-down, we somehow find a way to rip the soul from one another. It's a small world after fucking all. I still can't believe it really. Did he really sleep with the two of them at once the day before he married me?

I'm nuts, hurt, torn, angry, confused. So many thoughts are going through my head. I'm trying to be calm about it all, but I'm mad as hell! I want a divorce! I don't. I do. I don't know. I love him. I hate him. I despise him. I feel sorry for him. I love him again. I hate him even more. He makes me sick. He can go to hell!

But wait, no! I still want him. He's still my husband. Why did I marry him? My heart. My life. My soul mate. The one I dream for. Bastard! Liar! Muthafucka! Stupid ass! But I need him! If forgiving him this time buys my ticket into Heaven, then I'd rather go to hell! Asshole! But he needs me! Damn! That dick! Shit! Dumb ass! How could he?

Damn, I slept with Shawn. He felt so good, but Shawn? Oh God, too much! I need a drink! I want my Mommy!

Jay Z's still *Big Pimpin'* on the floor attached to my jeans. The cell phone is ringing again. Tears fall from my eyes.

Amazingly, I don't feel like I've committed incest. Shawn is the closest to a real-life brother that I've ever had. Yet I don't feel disgusted for sharing myself with him. I've never betrayed Khalil before. But making love to Shawn somehow felt right, comforting, and real. I belonged in his arms. I feel so safe with him, so warm, so protected; he made me feel so good, so loved, wanted and needed. And yes, I love him for that.

"Baby?" Shawn speaks. His head still on my chest listening to my heartbeat. I'm almost afraid to answer, but I need to.

"Yes, Shawn?"

Shawn turns his head to face me, still using my breasts as his pillows. I prop myself up so that I can look down at him. He's gorgeous, but I never looked at him this way until now. Shawn smiles at me and kisses my breast.

"What do we do now, Amber?"

Something inside of me wants him to continue to kiss me, caress me.

"I don't know Shawn. Nothing makes sense to me anymore."

I rub his head and gently glide my fingers over his temple, down the profile of his handsome face, trace his lips with my fingertips. He can see that I'm starting to well up again. He gets up and hugs me. I'm resting in his arms as he wipes my tears away and bends down to kiss my lips. I look up at him.

"Shawn, I'm so hurt."

He runs his hands through my hair then embraces me steadily.

"I'm hurt too, Amber. I found out some things in Virginia, well at least, I suspect some serious things, and I didn't want to bother you with them earlier. I need to talk to you, baby girl."

I'm prepared to listen to everything Shawn has to tell me, but I'm distracted. I can't help but to replay the session in my mind. Shawn is such a different lover than Khalil. He's gentle, and his strokes come with a different history behind them. His kisses, carnal. His passion, intense. His moans, even his language in bed...the way he talked to me, held me, caressed me, licked, kissed, and sucked, how he dug so deep...it's inappropriate to think of it, really, but it makes me want to know him better in this way. I love Khalil, but Shawn has my heart right now.

How does one explain this? How is it even possible? As I lay here in his arms, my head now rests on his chest, and I want like hell to make love to him once more, no matter how wrong it is. I imagine I'm just in some sort of weird natural state.

Shawn must be reading my mind, as he looks deep into my eyes. All reason leaves him as he kisses me fervently once more. I straddle him as if I'm going to ride him. Both of our breathing becomes heavy and hectic as he licks my lips, my neck, cups both my breasts into his hands, and sucks on my nipples.

I'm ready to cum all over again, but I can't. Oh God, he's fine! I'm confused. Should I stop? Why should I? He felt so good! What about Khalil? Fuck That! *Khalil who?* Damn! I'm supposed to be here. This is *my* time. No more pain, hurt, agony, or betrayal. From now on, I look out for number one...Me!

This man with me...Shawn, my husband's best friend, his right hand man, his dawg, his brother, his homey, his partner, his side-kick, his boy, his road-dog, his ace, his peeps...I know he loves Khalil, but right now, he's lovin' me more.

Shawn's dick is getting hard again. I can't do this again, but I want to. Need to. It's the easiest thing to do. Can't confront reality. He's so sweet. I love him. I don't. I do. I don't know. Shawn's phone rings.

"Are you going to get that, Shawn?" The constant ringing of Shawn's loft phone disturbs our peace in the storm and brings us closer to our inevitable reality.

"No, Amber. I don't feel much like talking to anyone right now. All I wanna do is be here. With you." Shawn kisses my lips once more. I get up from the bed and wrap myself in his sheet, head to the window, and peak through the blinds. The answering machine comes on, and an all too familiar voice resonates loudly.

"Yo Shawn, man, listen. I don't know where Amber is, man. I'm going crazy Shawn. I came home; she's not here. I called her mother; she's not there. Talked to Keisha, and she hasn't heard from her all day. Keisha had a stink attitude with me on the phone, I think she knows something too. I even called Scott's punk-ass, and he hasn't talked to her either. Shawn, man, I'm real scared. When she called me, she was crying hard as hell. I think she found out about the bachelor party, man! How could I

be so fucking stupid, man? What the fuck was I thinkin' about?
Oh God Shawn, if I lose her again, I don't know what I'll do, yo.
Call me back, man. Please. If she calls you, man, tell her I love
her. You gotta help me, Shawn. You gotta fix this for me, man. I'm
goin' crazy, yo. Call me when you get this message."

Beeeeeep.

Once again, I'm frozen at the window. I'm wrapped in nothing
but Shawn's sheet, naked in Shawn's bedroom, and the tears fall
again. Shawn walks over to me, hugs me from behind, moves my
hair to one side, and rests his chin on my shoulder. He kisses me
on my cheek, like the old Shawn used to. It no longer feels like a
brother kissing his sister.

"Amber, we'll get through this. But, I'm afraid that at this
moment, I'm not the voice of reason. Amber, what we shared
today made me realize that I've always loved you." Shawn stops
speaking and turns me to face him.

"Amber, look at me. I'm torn. I feel real fucked up but happy
at the same time. I've come to realize that I know you better than
any woman in my life. And, you know me, too. We've connected
over the years without even knowing it. Please, Amber, tell me
you feel the same way."

Oh God, this is too much. Shawn's not thinking clearly. Yes,
he's been my shoulder, my confidant, my rock even, but I've
never looked at Shawn quite like this before. Making love to him
has made me feel like I've been missing out on something my
entire life. Yes, Khalil is a great lover, but Shawn's lovemaking
was spiritual, almost God-fearing.

"Amber, say something, please. Do dreams come true?
Because I dream of you!" he begs.

"I don't know what to say Shawn. Right now, nothing makes
sense to me anymore." I understand this is not what Shawn wants
to hear. But I refuse to lie to him. There have been too many lies.

I do love him, but I can't love him the way he deserves. *Does that make any sense at all?* I love my husband, but I hate him, too. Torn is an understatement at this point.

"We need to talk, Amber. There are some things that I need to share with you."

My tears are still falling, because I feel that Shawn does love me. *How did I get into this mess?* I can't begin to address this right now.

"Shawn, we can't deal with that right now." I play with the blinds, peeking out again to see the pedestrians walking the streets of Manhattan. I pretend as if I'm sincerely interested in what's going on down below.

"I know, Amber, but please listen. I think Aaliyah is Shayla's sister." Shawn hands me a photograph and continues. "I know that sounds strange, but Lexis showed me this picture of her and her *'Auntie Lee Lee.'* This is the reason I had Aaliyah go to the spa today. I needed to be alone when I came home. I needed time to sort things out in my mind, make sense of it all. I never got into it with you about how Aaliyah and I met, because I never wanted you to think less of me. I never wanted you to pass judgment on Aaliyah, without getting to know her. But I met Aaliyah one day at the modeling agency Shayla was working at part time. Neither of them said anything about being related in any shape, form or fashion. I still can't understand either one of their agendas. Maybe it's totally innocent, but since Shayla is involved, I doubt it. I just need some time to get this straight in my head."

I listen to the words that are coming from Shawn's lips and stare at the picture in my hand. I still can't fully comprehend what he's just said. Aaliyah and Shayla? No way! Shayla is a vindictive, shiesty bitch, but that's Shayla. Khalil is such a stupid ass. But why Aaliyah? I try to give her the benefit of the doubt.

"Maybe Aaliyah couldn't find a way to tell you, Shawn? Maybe she was scared or something?" I'm trying to make Shawn feel better, but that bitch definitely has something up her sleeve. Aaliyah doesn't know the wonderful man she has in Shawn, with her stupid ass.

"No, Amber. Aaliyah knows she can talk to me about anything. When I felt like I wanted to marry her, I made that clear. I told her in the beginning...no secrets, no lies, we're in this together. Something's up, Amber, and I can't figure it out. In addition to this, I need to figure out how to talk to Khalil. What do I say to my best friend? That I'm in love with his wife? That he should've done right by her? Do we keep this a secret, Amber?"

"I don't know what to think, say nor do, Shawn. I just don't know if I can go through this again with Khalil. I love him so much Shawn, but, but..."

My tears overwhelm me and I am no longer able to speak.

"But what, Amber?" Shawn grabs me tighter. I try to respond to tell him that.....*I do love him too.* "What were you going to say Amber? That you still want to be with Khalil? Go ahead and say it, Amber. I know you do. You've loved that man so hard for so long. He doesn't know how fucking lucky he is to have you. I try to tell him that all the time, Amber. He's blessed to have you. So go ahead and say it. No sense in holding anything back, not now...we've already crossed the line, been past the point of no return. Talk to me, Amber. Don't shut down on me now. You've never had a problem confiding in me before."

"Shawn jus'....jus'....just forget about it." I try like hell to rid my face of the tears, but it's no use. No sooner do I move my hand away, more tears are waiting to cross the picket line. "Shawn, I feel like I need a drink. Would you mind making one for me? I just need something to take the edge off."

"Alright, Amber, I could use a drink, too. Anything to help me cope...help us get our heads right." Shawn walks down the stairs, and I think I hear the doorbell ring. I'm so consumed with my own drama that I can't really tell or care.

My cell phone rings again and instead of avoiding the problem once more, I decide to confront my fears. I open the flip and speak.

"Hello?" The voice on the other end of the phone brings a smile to my face as well as some relief to my existence.

"Baby girl? What the fuck is going on? You okay? And why the hell is your husband calling *me* looking for *you*?" Scott's voice, although serious right now, relaxes me a little.

"Scott, please. Just slow down so I can explain."

"Explain?" Scott persisted. "Explain, what? How your husband interrupted my groove? I'm way over here at Chi-Chi's, in the village, when Khalil rings my phone, not once, but twice, looking for you. He sounded real nervous and not at all in control, called himself questionin' me about you. Askin' me shit like, when was the last time I spoke to you or if I'd seen you today. But when I asked him what the problem was, he ain't wanna talk no more. So I politely told your *huzbin'* that if he couldn't answer my question, I damn sure wasn't answerin' his. Trust me, baby girl, the *only* reason I decided to call you is because Khalil *never* calls me so I knew something was wrong. I didn't call you for him, but for me. I had to make sure you were okay, so spill it." *Khalil really did call Scott.*

My tears well up again as I begin to confide in Scott.

"Scott, listen," I muster between sobs. "So much has happened and…."

"Hold up! Are you *crying*?" Scott interrupts me as I try to explain. "Did that black, fake ass Tyrese, Tyson Beckford wannabe put his hands on you? Baby girl, just say the word and

I *swear* I'll have my peoples hunt his ass down and have him assassinated. You hear me? See, this some bullshit right here. Let me get the fuck outta this club. Got me in here sweatin' like a whore in confession. Baby girl, gimme half an hour and I'll be right there!"

"Scott, no!" I yell, trying to get his attention. "It's nothing like that, Khalil would never put his hands on me."

"You sure, Amber?" Scott insists. "Cause you know us queens have been known to make muthafuckas disappear."

The thought of Scott and his *peoples* inflicting bodily harm on Khalil makes me smile. I know he's only looking out for me, but Scott knows he wouldn't hurt a fly. I try to reassure him that Khalil didn't touch me.

Scott continues. "And did you know Khalil even called that "N*egro spiritual*" Keisha looking for you. I know because Keisha called me so he must've made her nervous as well. Amber, where are you?"

"Scott, I'm at Shawn's house in Manhattan. Listen honey, so much has happened. Let me start at the beginning."

Scott interrupts again. "Amber, did he hurt you? I'll castrate that son of a bitch with the swiftness."

"Scott, *please*, let me tell you. Khalil and Shawn went to Virginia because Khalil's daughter Lex had a recital. I found out that he was going from Aaliyah, the morning of, which really upset me."

I should have known yet another interruption was due.

"What the fuck? See, I told you about that lily-white bitch, Aaliyah. She didn't smell right once I got to know her stinking ass. Bet she couldn't wait to call and tell you that shit. Some bitches just love being the bearers of bad news. To see Lex, huh? Oh, that lil' bastard chile of his? And he wasn't gonna tell you, huh? Oh see…"

I plead for Scott to hear me out. "Scott, please. I encouraged Khalil to go, because you know he doesn't give that child enough time. He has not been anything near the father he should be to that little girl. Besides, she didn't ask to be here. She has two stupid ass parents that were irresponsible."

"Okay, so why didn't he tell you he was going? If it was only concerning his daughter, why'd you have to hear it from the fatal attraction?"

I smile again because Scott always has a way of defining people. "I don't know, Scott. He said he was just waiting for the right time to tell me. And when I think about it, there's no way he could've left town without telling me. But when Aaliyah told me about it, it just threw me, because I never saw it coming. He barely even talks about Lexis."

"All the more reason he should of said something. I'm more than sure his trip wasn't no spur of the moment shit. He had to know about it for weeks and he ain't say nuthin'? Some men are so fuckin' stupid, creatin' unnecessary drama for no fuckin' reason at all."

"Anyhoo, Scott, that's history. But listen. Keisha and I went to see Miss Beverly earlier today, you know, my favorite patient at the nursing home? She had a stroke and she's in UMDNJ. Scott, believe me when I tell you it's a small fucking world, because it turns out that Miss Beverly's granddaughter is Loreatha a.k.a. *Chyna*, your friend Eva's partner."

"What?" Scott jumps in. "Chyna's real name is Loreatha?" Scott busts out with uncontrollable laughter. "Oh, no bitch! Just wait 'til I tell er'body this bullshit."

"Would you shut up and let me finish boy!" I respond, frustrated.

"Long story short, Scott. Chyna saw my wedding photo that I'd brought to the hospital for her grandmother. Turns out, her and Eva fucked Khalil at his bachelor party!" The thought of them with my husband makes me cry again. No matter how hard I try, I can't keep from bawling my eyes out. To describe Khalil's indiscretions to someone else hurts like hell. It constantly replays in my mind, over and over again. There's dead silence on the other end of the phone.

"Scott? Hello? Are you still there?"

"Yeah, I'm here, Amber." Scott's tone sounds almost as sorry as I am. "I just can't believe this shit. Honey, trust me, as of right now, Eva and Chyna are both officially out of business. See, them bitches didn't realize they were fucking with family now...and my sister at that? Oh, believe me, baby girl. Consider their lives officially ruined. They'll be ran out of Jersey by week's end. Their dick-sucking privileges have officially been revoked!"

"Scott?" I continue hesitantly. I know I can tell him anything, but I feel like what I'm about to say will destroy his faith in me. "Please don't share what I'm about to say with anyone. Please? Not even Keisha, okay?"

"You know I won't say anything, Amber. What is it?"

"You know that you and Keisha are my best friends, and I love you both dearly, so please don't look at me differently once I tell you this."

I can hear Scott breathing heavily through the phone. "Amber, what is it? You're scaring me!"

I hesitate for a moment, and then proceed with my confession. "I was too embarrassed to talk to you and Keisha about the Khalil episode, so I called Shawn. Well actually, I came over here to his house. I didn't know what else to do. He's always been the shoulder I cried on with Khalil's madness and..."

The tears gush forward, making it too hard for me to continue. What do I say at this point? That I slept with my husband's best friend? That I allowed Shawn to love me in ways Khalil has never thought of?

"Amber, stop crying." Scott continues, trying to calm me down. "Whatever it is, baby girl, you can tell me. What's so bad that it's making you feel this way?"

I suddenly get the nerve to continue. Scott's one of my best friends and maybe if I'd gone to him or Keisha first, none of this would have ever happened. "Scott, I slept with Shawn," I blurt out between sniffles. "I didn't plan it, Scott, it just happened. I'm so sorry, Scott, I know this is not me. I don't know what came over me. But at the time, it just seemed right. Shawn found out some things about Aaliyah, and everything just came down on us at once. I guess he was vulnerable, feeling betrayed. I was vulnerable, feeling betrayed, and it just happened. I feel so ashamed. I've never betrayed Khalil, ever. This person in my body is not me, Scott. I'm not this woman. I'd never do anything remotely close to what I've done. It doesn't make any sense. Nothing makes any sense. What have I done, Scott?"

"Listen, Amber," Scott responds gravely. "I love you like a sister, with all my heart and soul, bitch, you hear me? You can *always*, and *should* come to me with anything. And I'm sure Keisha feels the same way. Don't you *ever* feel embarrassed about anything with me. We've been a part of each other's lives for too long, been through too much. As for the Shawn episode, I won't sugarcoat anything and you know that. Yes, Amber, you were wrong. Dead fucking wrong! Despite the fact that Khalil is a dirty dick muthafucka, you were supposed to remain true as long as you share his last name. Never allow the indiscretions of another to force *you* out of character. Once you do, you've allowed them to win. I know you need me right now, and I'm here for you. You know me. I've always been a realist, and I never bite my tongue. You should know I'm not gonna start now.

Girl, Shawn is a great friend to you and a superhero to your dumb-ass husband. And yes, if I thought I could get him, I would have taken a run at him by now. I've always admired the way he treats you with so much respect. He treats everyone that way, because he's a nigga with class. But, baby girl, if all this has happened, the way you say it has, then Shawn has and always will be in love with you, Amber. Aaliyah was just the skank to make him realize that."

Damn. Scott is on a roll.

"From the first moment I met *good-ole Shawnny*, I could tell you were with the wrong man. You know I can smell any scent a person emits. Nothing gets pass me, especially when it comes to you. Shawn loves you honey. And as fucked up as it is, I think…you love him too. But just remember this little thing called karma. I'm a firm believer in it. What goes around, comes around, you hear me?"

Oh God! Scott's words add an even new dimension to the pain, betrayal and total confusion. *Could he be right? I would think that I should know who I'm in love with, right? I can't tell anymore, not right now. Where is Shawn with that drink?*

I prepare to respond to Scott, when I suddenly realize that Shawn is taking a mighty long time to bring our drinks. I *really* need one bad right now. Still wrapped in Shawn's sheet, I head downstairs to see what's taking Shawn so long, still keeping the phone prompt to my ear. Funny how I don't give a shit if Aaliyah steps through the front door or not. This is really not like me, but I'm so fucked up at the moment, that I could really care less about anything. Not anymore.

I walk to the top of the stairs and prepare to walk down, when I suddenly drop the phone over the top railing. The phone crashes at the bottom and breaks into a million tiny pieces on the living room floor. It's funny, but I don't even hear the sound it makes when it hits.

My heart stops, then races. I feel faint, weak, dizzy even. I wanna die right now, no matter how I get there; I'm ready to meet my maker in the worst way. My heart has somehow managed to ascend to my throat. I'm shaking and in a cold sweat. I feel like I'm in one of those nightmares where you're running for your life, screaming, trying to wake up, but you can't. I'm crying, screaming, but no one can hear me. I'm dying inside. My words are forming but nothing's coming out of my mouth.

Apparently, the doorbell did ring, as Shawn and Khalil are at the bottom of the stairs talking. Khalil looks up at me, his wife, naked, wrapped in his best friend's sheet, in his best friend's loft, coming down his best friend's stairs, after making love to his best friend. Time stops. All I can see is the confusion and rage in Khalil's face as he looks up at me. His rage turns to sorrow as his eyes fill with tears. I see him lip sync the words, "*Amber! No!*" No sound escapes those lips, and I can't hear anything. All is happening in slow motion.

Shawn, shirtless, and wearing only sweats, tries to calm Khalil down but Khalil, in turn, punches Shawn and he falls to the floor. My pace quickens as I rush to the bottom of the stairs. No longer do I feel the floor beneath me. All I can think of is reaching Shawn, reaching my husband, stopping the madness.

Khalil gets on top of Shawn and punches him repeatedly in his face, yelling all types of things. Again, I see his mouth moving, but I hear nothing. I'm deaf, I'm mute, and I wish I were blind as well.

Shawn breaks free of Khalil's hold. He overpowers him and pins Khalil to the floor. Severe blows erupt from Shawn's fists and lands on Khalil's jaw. Both of their noses are bleeding—lips swollen and busted. *Oh God, I can't believe this.* My hearing comes back to life, however, I hear only my own screams as I reach the two of them.

"No! Stop it! Shawn! Khalil! Stop it! No! Please!" I cry hysterically and try like hell to break the two of them apart. "Shawn. Khalil. Please stop it!"

Shawn looks up at me with hurt in his eyes, then looks back to Khalil. Tears fall from his eyes as he releases his hold on Khalil. Khalil has other plans.

Without warning, Khalil uses the lower palm of his hand and hits Shawn in his nose. Shawn falls backward onto the floor, holding his nose and shaking his head, trying to regain his balance. Khalil wastes no time in climbing back on top of Shawn and finishing where he left off. More punches are thrown.

Khalil stands and stomps Shawn in his abdomen. Shawn grabs hold of Khalil's foot and kicks him in the groin. Khalil falls to the floor and the two of them switch places, yet again. Shawn climbs on top of Khalil, instead of hitting him, he pleads.

"That's enough, Khalil!" Shawn screams as he pins Khalil down by the arms. "I don't wanna hurt you, man! Just listen to me!"

Khalil ignores Shawn and tries to free himself. He's no match for Shawn's strength. Shawn continues to beg. "Please, K, stop! Let me explain, man. I never meant to hurt you! I love you, man, please, just listen to me!"

All the while, I stand idly by the two of them, I am frozen and unable to move. At this point, Niagara Falls is no match for my tears. I'm screaming, crying and making no sense at all. This is all my fault, no one to blame but me. Scott was right. Karma is a muthafucka!

I will myself to move from the spot my feet have grown so attached to. I manage to take my arms and pull Shawn off Khalil, and he doesn't resist my force. Khalil stands and rage still consumes him and all I can see in his eyes, his soul. He takes a step toward Shawn, and I position myself between them. My back is against Shawn's stomach; I extend my hand as it touches Khalil's chest.

"Khalil, please," I cry out. "No more. Please stop."

Khalil looks into my eyes, then at the sheet wrapped around me. He then gives me a look as if he's never seen me before in his life. Tears run down his face. He grabs my hand from his chest and pulls me away from Shawn closer to him.

I don't know why but I'm not afraid. Something inside of me *wants* him to take me in his arms. And at the same time, something inside of me *needs* Shawn to pull me back.

"What did you do, Amber?" Khalil cries. "Please tell me I didn't lose you."

Inside, I scream, *No you haven't lost me, and nothing happened, I love you Khalil, you're my husband, and I'd never betray you.* Instead, I don't speak. Somehow, I feel as if there's nothing left to say. How can I forgive him this time? Do I really expect him to forgive me?

"Amber, I love you." Khalil's voice intensifies. "I'm sorry baby, please. It was a mistake. It meant nothing to me. Baby, think about it, we weren't even married when it happened, baby, please. You have to forgive me. We weren't even married."

I remove myself from Khalil's grasp and take a step back. *Oh, No! He didn't just say that shit.* All of the hurt, the pain, the lies, the cries, the sleepless nights, the turmoil, the forgiveness, the unforgivable, and the entire process even, come back into play.

I take my right hand, with all the years of bullshit and betrayal behind it, and slap the living daylights out of Khalil. I smack the shit, the hell and the damn out of him! His head snaps to one side from my blunt force and remains there. I'm not sure, but I think his neck cracked. I wish I could find it inside of me to slit his throat for how angry I am. However, I do manage to make this much clear.

"You weren't married, huh? So that gave you the right to fuck two bitches at once, the night before you married me? After all we've been through Khalil?" I slap him again. "I've always been true to you. I've forgiven you for everything, every time. But do you know that this bitch, who by the way, knows your corny, childish-ass signature statement, "get your swallow on," even gloated about fucking you? Fucking my man? My husband? She bragged about it Khalil! She boasted about drinking you down *to the last drop*! Do you know the humiliation I've endured behind your escapades? Do you? And you do this in the name of love? Go to hell Khalil! Go to muthafuckin' hell!"

Khalil drops to his knees, grabs my legs into his arms. "Amber, I'm so sorry. Please, Amber. Take as much time as you need, but baby, please don't leave me, I can't live without you, Amber. You are the reason I can do anything, baby, please, Amber."

Shawn interrupts, still the gentleman he's always been. "Listen…"

"Fuck you, Shawn!" Khalil interrupts. "You s'posed to be my dawg, man, my right hand man. Fuck you, man!"

"Listen, Khalil," Shawn insists. "I love you like a brother, and I know I fucked up big time, man. I know you'll never be able to forgive me, man, and I'm willing to live with that for the rest of my life. Bottom line is....you have the most beautiful woman here with you, who loves you dearly, and as much as it pains me to say it, she doesn't love me man. Not the way she loves you, anyway."

"What the fuck are you talking about, Shawn?! Are you trying to tell me about *my* wife? You think you know *my* wife better than *me*?!"

"I'm not saying that, Khalil. I'm just pointing out the obvious to you. What happened between Amber and I wasn't planned, it just happened. I never intended to hurt either of you, and I'll understand if neither of you ever want to see me again."

"You fuckin' right we never want to see you again, BITCH!" Khalil screams at the top of his lungs. "You can drop dead for all I fuckin' care! You call yourself my friend? My brother? You stood next to me when I took my vows and this is what you do? *Fuck* my wife? What did you do, Shawn? Invite her to cry on your punk ass shoulder, then abuse her when she was most vulnerable? Tell me, *brother*, did you make my wife cum? You a ladies' man, right? You treat 'em all with respect, right? Were you respecting my wife while you were fuckin' her? All that shit you talk about being a man and playing your position, was all bullshit, Shawn! You ain't shit to me....nothing! If I saw your ass layin' in a ditch, on fire, I wouldn't piss on your bitch ass! Fuck you, nigga, and if you ever come near me or my family again, I swear, I'll fuckin' kill you!"

The look on Khalil's face tells me he's serious. I don't believe I've ever seen this side of him before. Sure, I've witnessed him angry, but never like this. Suddenly, he looks at me with hate in his eyes, the epitome of all that is evil. His mouth is still moving, but my deafness returns. I can't hear what he's saying.

His arms are grabbing me, pulling me, but I don't know what he wants. I try desperately to focus, but I can't. Everything around me goes black, and I'm lost in space. I panic as I try to find my way back, but it seems so far away. Faintly, I hear Shawn and Khalil's voices calling me in the darkness. I can't get to them; I can't find them. I search desperately but it's no use, as I float further and further away.

"Amber." Khalil calls out my name; his voice seems clearer, closer. "Amber, baby, wake up."

I open my eyes. Khalil is standing over me. I look around and see that I'm still in Shawn's loft, laying on the couch. But how the hell did my clothes get back on? Who dressed me? And why doesn't Khalil have a scratch on him? And where's Shawn?

"You okay, Amber?" Khalil continues trying to get a response from me.

What the hell is going on? I sit up on the couch. Everything in the room spins. My head feels as if Plymouth Rock has landed on it. I place my head in my hands and still can't help but wonder how I managed to get dressed without remembering. And again, where the fuck is Shawn?

Abruptly, Shawn enters the living room with aspirin in one hand and water in the other and hands them both to Khalil.

"Thanks, man, for looking out for her 'til I got here."

Khalil speaks calmly to Shawn, then looks at me.

"Here Amber, take this, it'll make you feel better." I take the aspirin from him and chase the pills with water. *What the hell is going on here?* Shawn doesn't have a scratch on him either. Why the hell are the two of them acting as if nothing happened?

"No problem, man." Shawn is fully clothed. "That's what friends are for. You know I'll look out for my baby sis anytime."

Okay, enough is enough. Something's going on here and I feel as if I've just woke up in the Twilight Zone.

"What's going on?" I ask both of them, hoping to get some sort of explanation. But instead of answering me, they both look at each other and laugh in unison. Khalil sits down next to me and rubs my hair away from my face.

"Baby, you passed out." Khalil continues while smoothing my hair back. "I called Shawn a little while ago, and he told me you were here. He said you showed up here, a mess, crying real hard and he couldn't make out a word you were saying. Then he said, you went into the den and started drinking like a fish, just mixing everything you saw, and drinking it. He said you were acting neurotic, like a crazed person, and he got scared. He said he tried grabbing you, tried to get you to calm down, but you wouldn't listen. Eventually, you stopped all on your own....well, you passed out here on his couch."

I take my focus from Khalil and look over at Shawn who's sitting on his loveseat. Is this shit for real? Was anything for real?

Khalil continues telling me his accounts of things.

"Amber, I know we need to talk. When you called me a few hours ago, asking me about the bachelor party, I knew you'd found out. But listen to me, Amber, please. None of that meant anything. You gotta believe me baby, when I tell you I love *you* and *only* you. It's *always* been you. I'm so sorry for anything I've ever done to hurt you, and if I could take it all back, I would. But please, Amber, listen to me when I tell you that I would do anything for you. Without you, there's no me, there's no place for me, no use for me. Without you, I don't exist, can't exist, and won't exist. This past weekend in Virginia, I missed you like crazy, baby, I couldn't wait to get home to you. I told Shayla that there are going to be a lot of changes. Changes that involve Lexis and not her. Amber, baby, nothing matters more to me than you and my daughter, and if you'll allow it, I want us to be a family. Please, Amber, just think about everything I've said. I know it'll probably take time for you to really hear me out, but I know exactly what I want now, know exactly what I need, and that's you. I took a vow to spend the rest of my life with you, so please, Amber, don't throw that all away."

Khalil finishes and kisses me on my lips. I swear I'm trippin'. An hour or so ago, I was upstairs making love to Shawn. Wasn't I? Did I dream all of that? The lovemaking? The fight? I couldn't have been dreaming. It was all so real, so life-like. I felt Shawn inside of me, I still feel him, his kisses, his touch, and his breath on my neck, his smell even. No, I couldn't have been dreaming. Am I going crazy? What's happening to me? I get up from the couch and walk toward the kitchen. I stagger a bit before I get my balance. Both Shawn and Khalil reach for me.

"Let me help you, baby." Khalil gets to me first as I stand up from the sofa.

"Why don't you sit down, Amber. Whatever you need, I'll get it for you."

"No, Khalil," I hazily respond, confused. "I need to go to the bathroom."

Shawn comes over and takes one of my arms, while Khalil holds the other. *Damn, what was I drinking?* I can barely stand and my legs feel like rubber. And why are my thighs sore? The two of them help me into the bathroom outside the den and I assure them that I can handle it from here. I manage to get my pants down and notice that my panties are on inside out. I sit down on the toilet and feel the moisture between my legs, but I have not yet done anything. I unroll the tissue and wipe myself, almost afraid to look at it, but I do. I bring the tissue closer into view and observe the remnants of Shawn. I exhale.

I stagger from the bathroom and find Shawn sitting in the living room alone.

"Where's Khalil?" I ask, wondering why Shawn has such a serious look on his face.

"He had to park down the street when he got here, so he went to bring the truck closer so you wouldn't have to walk. He said that he's going to order dinner for the two of you from the Jamaican restaurant down the street, then he'll be back."

Shawn gets up from the sofa and moves closer to me. "Come on, Amber, let me help you outside."

Shawn grabs me around my waist. I place one arm around his neck. I notice the scratches that are so deeply embedded in his neck. I stop in my tracks and turn to face him.

"Shawn, wait a minute." I proceed, still confused about the past accounts. "What's going on, Shawn? A couple of hours ago, we were...."

"Amber, don't," Shawn interrupts me and kisses me passionately. His tongue tastes familiar as it swims around in my mouth. "If you don't leave now, Amber, I'm afraid I won't let you leave later. It's going to be hard for me to let you go."

"But Shawn, how did I....?"

Shawn pushes me back into the bathroom. Closes the door softly and locks it. He bends me over the sink aggressively, but not forcefully.

"Shawn…!"

He parts my legs with his knees, pulls my pants down and proceeds to bite my ass, lick my cheek, and trace his tongue up the small of my back. I feel the rain coming again. He takes his left hand and reaches around to grab my face gently, pulling me back toward him. I feel him solid through his sweats as he presses up against me. He pulls me further into his chest and whispers in my right ear.

"Amber, I will always love you. You know that? I've loved you since the days I first laid eyes on you, baby." Shawn takes his right hand, reaches around and puts his fingers in my wetness. He feels how saturated I've become. He exhales deeply and pulls his fingers up to both of us. "You see this. This is me all in you. And the remains of what you and I shared. I love it."

He places those fingers in my mouth to give me a taste. I lick them. I'm moaning.

"You love it too, Amber, don't you?"

I can't help myself. "Yes, Shawn, I love you. I love it. Everything about you, I do."

He turns me around so that now I am face to face with him. Licking my lips once, then twice, then kissing my neck, he pushes me away.

"Amber, go, now. Because I swear if you don't leave right now, I'll never, ever let you go. Just go, baby." I try to speak, but Shawn places his finger over my lips. "Just go, Amber."

"Shawn, what about...?"

"I dressed you, Amber." Shawn continues with explanation. "After we finished making love, we started drinking. You were crying so much, that it bothered me so I gave you something to help you sleep. I didn't want Khalil to find you like that, so I dressed you and carried you back downstairs. This is your life, Amber, and it's not for me to decide who you're going to be with. I love you, Amber. I meant that when I said it earlier and nothing's changed."

"But what about the fight?"

"What fight? What are you talking about?"

"You and Khalil. You two were fighting right here in the living room. You were bleeding, he was bleeding, and I couldn't stop it."

Shawn looks at me and laughs. "No one was fighting, Amber. When Khalil got here, you were laying on the couch fast asleep. You must've dreamt that."

Was Shawn serious? Did I really dream that? It does make sense, though, especially since neither of them have a mark on them. I guess it's true when they say your dreams are usually about your fears, and or, your fantasies. I guess I was afraid that that's what would ultimately happen, once Khalil found out what I'd done.

As Shawn walks me to the front door, in walks Aaliyah, more beautiful than ever. I look at Shawn and remember what he said earlier about Aaliyah being Shayla's sister. The look in his eyes tells me that this is his fight and his alone.

Aaliyah looks at me and takes a stab at conversation but I ignore her. The thought of her trying to get between my legs makes me feel sick, and I'd like nothing more than to tell Shawn all about it. Just as I'm ready to expose her for the trifling bitch that she is, Khalil walks through the door.

"You ready, Amber?" Khalil reaches for me. "I moved the truck closer, so come on." Khalil takes me by the arm, but I'm finding it very difficult to release my hold on Shawn. For some reason, I feel I need to be here with him, take care of him, and defend him against the evil that has just entered his home.

"Wait a second, Khalil." I hesitate before leaving. "Let me talk to Aaliyah for a minute."

Khalil obliges and heads back outside. I turn to face Shawn, with Aaliyah standing by his side. I stare at her but speak to him. "Shawn, if you need me, I'll stay."

Aaliyah's cell phone rings. I flicker it lightly so that she loses the grip, and it falls to the floor. Shawn reaches down to the floor to pick it up. He places her cell on the coffee table and presses the speaker button.

"Lee Lee. What's going on? Khalil and Shawn left here. Khalil didn't even want to fuck me! Talkin' bout he love his wife too much and shit! Lee Lee, our plan didn't work! Dummy! I should tell Shawn everything...Hello? Hello?"

Shawn
Get to Steppin'

Aaliyah, stop calling me! I mean it!"
I can't believe this lyin' ass trick keeps calling me. It's been well over a month since our breakup and Aaliyah, in her mind anyway, believes that we are somehow meant to be together. She insists that she was forced by her sister, the infamous Shayla, to seduce me, with the hopes of ripping Amber and Khalil's marriage apart. What kind of tag-team are they? Did those two ghetto hood rats really think the shit would work?

"Look Aaliyah, I will tell you again, just like I told you last week, the week before, yesterday, ten minutes ago; it is over and there's not a damn thing you can do about it."

"But, Shawn, I'm trying to tell you that I had to do it! Please, Shawn, you have to understand that I had no choice. I love you, baby, please take me back," Aaliyah tells me as she cries like a baby on the other end of this phone. I smirk when I imagine how red her high-yellow ass must be after thirty minutes of continuous tear shedding. Smirk and all, she will not be getting back into my life, or my bed, ever.

During my time with Aaliyah, I thought I was a happy man, I really did. I felt so alive with her, was happy to have her on my arm, pleased to be her comforter and supporter. But the more I think about it, and the more I realize hindsight is twenty-twenty, the more I know that it wasn't meant to be. Momz always told me, "Always go with your first instinct. If something doesn't feel right, God blesses us with the ability to feel something deep down that serves as our sign, that it's no good for you. Follow your gut, baby." Hearing that from my mother so many times should've prepared me, and I should've gone with my gut instinct, but Aaliyah's beauty and seductive charm grabbed a hold of my heart, and loins, something serious, and I was weak. Shit, if I wasn't as strong as I am now...Aaliyah has the ability to make me fall for her all over again, well she did anyway. This experience, however, opened my eyes and made me realize what my trusty gut has told me for many years, that the true love of my life is my best friend's wife, Amber. What a dilemma.

Aaliyah's continuous sobs have become so commonplace that I drift off into another time and place, while she repeatedly screams, "Shawn, I love you! Please, Shawn!"

I remember that fateful day; the day I made love to Amber for the first time, which was also the day I threw Aaliyah's trifling, lying, dirty ass out of my home and life.

"Oh, you're getting the fuck outta here, Lee-Lee!"

"Shawn, why are you acting this way?" Aaliyah turned to face Amber on the front steps of the loft. Amber bent down to pick up the cell phone and handed it to Aaliyah, Shayla still on the other end screaming.

"Who's on the phone, Aaliyah? Your sister, Shayla?" Amber asked her, as she moves in so close to Aaliyah and forcing her to back up a few steps.

"Come on, Amber, let's go home. I don't need you around this skank ho!" Khalil said, while pulling Amber by the arm.

"No, you didn't call me a skank ho, Khalil! You got some fuckin' nerve, nigga. All the asses you done been up in, fucking anything that will open its legs. You bastard, you gots a lot of nerve!" Aaliyah was fuming.

"Aaliyah, you ain't got no room to talk about nobody. And damn right, I said it!" Khalil was screaming at the top of his lungs at Aaliyah, moving up another step to get closer to her. He leaned in, hovering over Aaliyah. "And should I tell Shawn how you tried to give me some pussy the other week? Prancing your stankin' ass around my man's loft, like you paid some fuckin' bills in this bitch. Trying to fuck his best friend. You just mad, I ain't wanna fuck your ass, bitch!"

I remember the look I gave Khalil after he made that comment about Aaliyah wanting to fuck him. It fucked me up for a minute, because I didn't see that coming. It fucks me up now, because I've done it to him. I fucked my boy's wife. Reflections won't leave my mind, although it's been some time. Aaliyah is still crying on the phone.

"Hello? Hello? Shawn? Are you still there?"

"Yes, Aaliyah, I'm still here. But I gotta go."

"Just give me another chance to explain. Can I come up there? I'll catch the train next weekend and meet you at the loft. I just want to explain, in person, Shawn, please, I love you so much."

Although Aaliyah's words seem sincere, I know they're not. She sang the same song that fateful day, and, without warning, her constant screams fade once again, and I go back to that day.

"Nigga, you know you wanted some of this ass. You just a punk-ass bitch, that's all," Aaliyah yelled back at Khalil. I stared at the both of them in disbelief. Amber

pushed Khalil back, got in Aaliyah's face to reveal her bombshell.

"So, does that make me a punk-ass bitch, too Aaliyah? You tried to fuck me too, but I didn't let you have none of this kitty kat. You a real sorry ass woman, Aaliyah. You and your sister. The both of you need help. You really do. Too bad my dumb ass husband couldn't stay away from your whore of a sister."

"Hello! Hello!" were the screams heard from Shayla on the phone. Everyone was so busy arguing that we forgot about the nucleus of all of this mess. Khalil snatched the phone from Aaliyah's hand and screamed into the receiver, "You a no good, bitch Shayla! How could you? I'm so sorry my daughter has such a fucked up mother."

Taking obvious offense to Khalil's last comment, Aaliyah hung up on Shayla, closed the phone tight, put it in her purse, and got into Khalil's face. "You don't ever speak to my sister that way again. You think you so smart, right, Khalil? You need to cotton swab your daughter's cheek, you stupid nigga!"

A screeching halt of a car, refocused all of our energy, as we looked toward the street to see what the problem was. Scott jumped out of a midnight blue Chrysler 300, while the car was still in motion, slamming the door behind him. Hurriedly, he walked to the front steps of the loft, throwing back his baby blue scarf, and removing his diamond studs in his ears. Placing the earrings into the pockets of his jeans, Scott frantically walked up the stairs, eyes only on Amber.

"Baby girl, you okay? Lord, I don't wanna have to murder no muthafuckas today. Help me, Lord."

"I'm fine, Scott."

Approaching Khalil, Scott looked him up and down. "You's a dirty dick having piece of shit, Khalil. You really gonna make me beat yo' ass one day, you hear me, black bastard!" Before Khalil *could get in a word, Scott refocuses his sight, along with his thoughts onto Aaliyah as he gradually stepped to her, carefully pointing his index finger into the middle of her forehead, pushing her head back, sending her a few steps backward. "Yeah, see, I knew something was up with your rotten ass, you lily-white bitch. Can't nobody have nuttin' nice with bitches like you around."*

"Look, Scott..."

SLAP!

Aaliyah couldn't get the remainder of her sentence to flow from her mouth, because Scott interrupted all thoughts and sayings from her, as he took his scarf off, let it drop to the ground, and proceeded to slap the shit out of Aaliyah, forcing her head to toss from one side to the next.

"See, bitch, don't say shit! I told you to stay away from my girl, Amber. That's what the fuck you get for not listenin'."

Yes, that was a day I will never forget. After that, I told Aaliyah to get to steppin'. And, everyday since, she's been calling, begging for a second chance.

"Shawn, please tell me it's okay to come and see you."

"Aaliyah, no it's not. Don't call here anymore. I told you once, twice, ten fucking times; it's over. I gotta go."

છ છ છ

The Bathwater...

If Aaliyah calls here once more, I think I may just have to go down to Virginia to pay her a visit, and slit her fucking throat. I get more and more anxious and aggravated each time I think about the shit she put me through. Getting Aaliyah and Amber, for that matter, out of my mind, heart, life and psyche ain't been an easy road. I pray to God, He gives me a much needed distraction. My conversations with God Almighty have been long and emotional lately. He's an awesome God.

The Devil quickly penetrates my thoughts and one of my episodes with Lee Lee comes to mind.

I walked in the front door of the loft, horny, devoted and I could almost taste Aaliyah. I'd been thinking about her all day and couldn't wait to get home to her. I grabbed at my dick and noticed it was already hard for her. As soon as I grab a quick shower, it's gonna be on and poppin' in here. I thought to myself.

Before heading up the stairs, I walked into the den and made myself a quick drink. A double shot of Henny warmed my insides as it made its way down easy. As I left the den and walked up the stairs, I heard Aaliyah's voice. I entered the bedroom without her seeing me and noticed she was on the phone.

"Hang up that phone baby," I whispered while hugging *Aaliyah from behind. "Who are you talking to anyway?"*

"Just a friend from back home," Aaliyah responded while *closing her flip and looking startled.*

I should've known something was up then. Damn, why didn't I see the warning signs? I began nibbling on her ear because I knew this was one of her erogenous zones and soon she'd be all over me.

"Not now, Shawn," Aaliyah huffed as she quickly put her *phone on vibrate.*

"C'mon Lee-Lee, it's been two days."

"I said not now! What the fuck do you want from me? And stop calling me that!" Aaliyah spit back at me.

I knew she hated when I shortened her name this way, but damn! I tried not to let her apparent attitude dissuade me so I continued with my foreplay.

"Is my bath water ready yet?" I asked while running my hands up her blouse and caressing her nipples.

Aaliyah knew that was my way of asking if she's wet enough for me. Normally, all I'd have to do is kiss her and my baby's ready but it seemed like something else was on her mind. She'd never dismissed me like that before.

"I'm sorry baby. It's just that I've got some things planned for the day. Maybe later I'll run your bath?"

"How much later?" I asked, disinterested in her plans. *"And what's so important that can't wait?"* I ignored her plea for me to pump my brakes and continued sliding my tongue down the nape of her neck.

Hindsight is always the clearest vision we have. And in hindsight, I should've known. I ain't never had to beg no woman for no ass, never in my life.

Suddenly, Aaliyah pushed away from me and yelled, "What is it that you don't understand Shawn?" Angrily she continues, *"No means fucking no!"*

"What the hell is your problem, Aaliyah?" I grew aggravated. *"You've been acting weird ever since the wedding."*

"What are you trying to say Shawn?" Aaliyah asked defensively.

"I'm not trying to say anything, I'm saying it! Is there anything you wanna tell me? Is there something I should know?"

I couldn't help but notice how Aaliyah's mood changed from agitated to panic.

"I'm talking to you Aaliyah, where the hell is your head right now?"

Her silence only added to my agitation and made my imagination run wild. Could she be cheating on me? I wondered. Oh, that pit in the stomach my momz warned me about. She never fought me like that in the past. But, I hadn't been with her that long either. What the hell's going on with her? All of a sudden, she didn't want to make love to me? I couldn't help but ask the only question feasible at that point.

"Aaliyah, is there another man?"

"No!" One word was her only response.

"Then what is it?" I insisted. "Is it something I did, something I said?"

"Shawn, I already told you that I have something to do." *Aaliyah continued while walking away from me. "That's all; it has nothing to do with you!"*

"No, that's not all." I raised my voice.

There, another sign. I never raise my voice at a woman.

"Something's going on Aaliyah! I can't touch you and your only explanation is you have something to do?" I grabbed her from behind and turned her to face me. "You haven't been yourself the last couple of days."

"Look, Shawn!" Aaliyah snatched away from me and reached for her sweater. "I have to go."

"You're not going anywhere, Lee-Lee!"

I responded while snatching her sweater from her. I knew she hated when I called her that but she was pissing me. On top of that, I wanted some pussy in the worst way! I can't help but laugh out loud right now!

I pushed her down on the bed and began ripping her clothes from her body. If she wanted me to fight for it, so be it! Aaliyah was a weirdo, so fighting her for some pussy seemed to go with the flow.

"This what you want?" I asked. "Does the nigga you creepin' with know how you like it?"

"Stop it Shawn, get off of me." Aaliyah pressed.

"Answer me, Lee-Lee." I insisted while I ripped her bra
from her body.

I knew sooner or later, she would have given in and let me
have my way. I knew how she liked to be chased. How much
it turned her on to be manhandled just a bit. I knew how much
she loved it when I took charge of the situation. You know....Be
the man and play my position. I quickly put her nipple in my
mouth, tugging, sucking, licking her breasts until they resembled
swollen chestnuts. My nature rose immediately.

But now that I think about it, it wasn't the kind of hard on
I like.

"Shawn, please," Aaliyah faintly whispered.

"Please what, Aaliyah?" I teased, knowing damn well she
couldn't resist me much longer. I had her skin tight jeans down to
her knees, but she had her legs bent, preventing me from taking
them all the way off.

"Please stop," Aaliyah sighed, out of breath. She knew her
strength was no match in comparison with mine. And I knew my
bath water had to be ready by then.

I still can't believe I begged that bitch and played those
childish games with her gutter ass.

"You want me to stop?" I asked out of breath while placing
my hand between her legs. Once I touched her there, it's over.
Why she made me go through the drama, I'll never understand.
I felt her moisture through her panties so I massaged her clit
without taking them off and listened to her moan.

"Mmmhhh," Aaliyah cried faintly. *"Shawn, no."*

It seemed like she was trying to fight me with everything
inside her but she should knew I wasn't going to stop. Couldn't
she feel my manhood pressing up against her? Didn't she
understand how badly I needed to be inside of her and only her?
She couldn't possibly have been serious about not giving it to

me, could she? No way. That bitch was purring like a kitty and wet like never before.

"Does no really mean no, Aaliyah?" I teased as I made the journey down to her hot spot. I finally got her jeans all the way off and ripped her panties to shreds as I spread her legs as far as I could. Before I began my feast, I fondled her inner thighs with kisses. And as my tongue spiraled toward her togetherness, Aaliyah could no longer resist. She simply closed her eyes and allowed me to take control.

"Damn baby, it feels so good." Aaliyah sang as she grabs my head. "This is how it's supposed to be."

"Shhhhh....don't speak." I whispered.

My tongue moved in and out...out and in. I dreamed of tasting her since I woke up that morning. Thinking of her goodness all day at work. Grabbing her ass and pulling her deeper in my mouth made the sensation for me so much more cosmic.

"Oh God!" Aaliyah screamed out.

My clitoral attack continued as I observed her back arching forward, welcoming every inch of tongue I had to offer. Moving in unison with my head, Aaliyah quivered in ecstasy. She knew this was what I loved to do to her. I smiled inside as I remembered just those moments ago when she tried to fight it. Sucking her like that was almost spiritual for me, considering she was going to be my wife.

"Fuck my face, Aaliyah." I couldn't help but whisper to her.

She obliged as if she was a hypnotized slave trying to please her master. Her moans became louder and her movements grew fierce! I felt her thighs tightening around my head. Grabbing her ass, I pulled her in closer. She fell forward, giving me more room to do my thing. My tongue plunged deeper, purposely providing more friction to her clit on the way in. Her inner core was drenched with moisture. I could tell the walls of her pussy were screaming for me to get inside.

I lift her up and laid her on her back. I ran my hands over her body and looked at how beautiful she was. I relished in the fact that she was all mine and I kissed her passionately. My hand made its way down to where my mouth had been and she opened her legs wider. Placing a single finger inside of her, we moaned in unison. I smiled at how wet she was and removed my finger and placed it in my mouth, then into hers. Aaliyah savagely lifted my shirt over my head and unbuckled my belt.

"You love me baby?" I asked as I took my pants all the way off.

"Yes." Aaliyah responded while pulling me back on top of her.

I kissed her long and hard before reaching down to put a condom on. Aaliyah tried to stop me from using a condom because she wanted it right then.

"We don't need that, Shawn." Aaliyah insisted as she tried to take the condom from my hand.

"Yes we do, baby." I reassured and smiled down at her, while opening the magnum with my mouth. I spit the remains of the black and gold wrapper onto the floor and quickly rolled the condom into place.

Now, I would never fuck Aaliyah without a hat on. My shit had to be wrapped up. Why? Maybe that was another sign. Damn.

My dick found its own way inside without any help. One stroke assured my entry and I felt the rain fall between her legs.

"Aaaahhh shit," I cried out as my man buried himself.

Her pussy was wet, but not that good and hot and nasty-fuck-your-life-up-wet like Amber's was. If I ever find some delicious ass sweet nectar like that on a good woman, shit, I will not be letting that shit go. I see why Khalil begged for forgiveness. But Aaliyah, it was just wet. I know this now, but then, you couldn't tell me shit.

Our bodies intertwined and formed a compatible rhythm as my manhood meshed and became one. I opened my eyes and looked down at her.

"Why'd you make me beg for it, Aaliyah?" I asked, breathing erratically.

"I didn't, Shawn," she responded, gazing back at me.

"You want me to stop?" I asked with seriousness, while reaching down and fondling her clit while still inside of her.

"Mmmmhh," she moaned.

"Answer me, Aaliyah." I persisted while massaging the massive lump between her legs and forcing myself in deeper.

"No, Shawn. Please don't stop."

I placed the palms of my hands on her inner thighs and pinned them down against the bed. I satisfied my urge to have her....to feel her warmth, her wetness flow uncontrollably. It was My pussy. I was ready to let go but was not ready to stop. She made me fight for it so I had to make it last as long as possible. Aaliyah dug her nails deep into my back and pulled me in deeper. I reciprocated and threw fight-like body shots, thrusting harder and faster.

"Aaaaahhhh" Aaliyah moaned.

"You cummin', baby?" I asked, with my own senses now disoriented and all reason gone with the wind.

It was just a fuck, now that I really think about it. Aaliyah was just a trophy on my arm, and a place to lay my pipe. She didn't love me, and I truly believe now that I never really loved her.

"Yesssssss."

I could only imagine that the pleasure she was experiencing

was as unbelievable as mine and I couldn't hold on any longer.

"I'm cummin' too, baby."

"Am…b…" Aaliyah yelled as she grabbed me tight enough to cut off my oxygen supply.

Was she screaming Amber? Ain't this a bitch!

Scott
Dickmatized

I can't believe this bitch is late again. What the hell I look like sittin' in this here restaurant, sippin' on a damn drink all by my lonesome? Lord knows, I gots better thangs to do. One of which, is to be sitting pretty, between the legs of Shane, Summer's brother and my new boyfriend.

I met Shane and Summer, right here at The Cheesecake Factory in Bergen County. Having just dropped a client off, I decided to stay for a drink, upon my client's insistence. That's when I saw him; Shane. I like to say it long and slow, for obvious reasons. Shaaaaaaaaannnnnnneeee! Ooh, damn. I remember that day, like it happened yesterday.

Our eyes met and begged for the chance to get to know one another. Well, at least that's what I felt. I rocked a crushed velvet tracksuit by some hot new designer, who gave it to me at a photo shoot. We won't mention what else little hottie gave me at the time. Then, he walked in; passion, love, deliciousness all wrapped up into one pretty, caramel coated package. I immediately jumped up from my seat at the bar, and walked over to him as he entered the restaurant. Sure, he had a woman by his side, but I didn't give a shit. I approached him, of course with a serious, fierce strut, and made myself known.

"Have we met?" I asked, looking him up and down, extending my hand to his for a shake. Oh my, I'm Dickmatized.

"I don't think so," he responded, adorably, in a beige pinstriped button up, with baggy khakis, and some pristine Rockport's; very neat and clean. He didn't need much to ignite my fire.

"Are you sure we haven't met?"

"Yes, I'm sure."

"Would you like to?"

"Like to what?"

"Meet."

"Sure."

"I'm Scott. Trust me when I tell you, the pleasure is all mine."

"Thanks Scott, I'm Shane. And this is my sister, Summer."

"Scott and Shane, perfect together."

"That's cute."

"You're cute."

A devilish smile escaped my lips, and he smiled. The kind of smile that made me want to drip in my drawers.

Yep, that's how my love came down, just like that old Evelyn "Champagne" King song. Me and Shane have been kickin' it ever since. Summer and I bonded something serious too. But, she 'bout to get the fuckin' boot, if she don't get her yellow ass in here soon. Speaking of yellow, I need to call Amber. But I'll have to do that later, here comes Miss Thang.

"So sorry I'm late, sweetie." Summer kisses me on each cheek.

"You know I was cussin' you out, bitch. You smell good, honey. What are you wearing?"

"I think it's *Beautiful* by Estee' Lauder."

"Whatever you're wearing, wear it more often, dear. And you look marvelous. Shed a few pounds, sista?"

"Just a few, Scott. I like being a woman with curves."

"I know that's right. You should see some of the models I work with, Summer. Size zeros, sweetie. No asses, no tits, nothing. And they call that shit sexy? Please."

"I know, Scott. I plan on staying in my size twelve. I'm quite comfortable here."

"Good for you."

"I took the liberty of ordering a Cosmopolitan for you. I know you love them."

"Thanks, honey. So what's new Scott?" She takes a sip, with curly hair flowing past her shoulders, and lips shining; glossy and pink. Summer reminds me of Amber sometimes.

"Not much. Same shit, different day. What's good with you?"

"Well, I need some help, Scott. With money."

"Summer, I don't do the money thing with anyone. Muthafuckas don't know how to pay shit back. Lend a nigga two dollars, and they disappear for two years."

Summer hits me on my shoulder and laughs out loud.

"Shit, I ain't laughin'. I'm tellin' you. I should write a book called, *Why Black Men Get 25 to Life.* I'll fuck you up for two dollars."

She's still doubled-over with laughter. But I am quite serious. But have to release a smile, 'cause this bitch about to pee on herself.

"No, Scott! I mean, I've been saving a little here and there, and over time, it's built up quite nicely."

"Oh, is that right? Well, sweetie. I can definitely help you in that department. I ain't got no problem spendin' a bitch's money. We can get started right now."

"Scott!"

"I'm jokin', girl. I have just the perfect person in mind to help you. He's a friend of a friend, and an investment banker. He's got his shit together too, girl, and will definitely be able to help you out."

"Oh, cool. Who is he?"

"Oooh, that question sent a quiver through my spine. I wish he was mine, that's who he is."

More laughter from Summer. Oh God, she has tears in her eyes. Let me tell the poor girl, before she has a conniption.

"His name is Shawn "Sexy Black Ass" Fontaine. Here's his number."

I take a napkin from the bar and write Shawn's number on it and hand it to Summer. Summer takes the napkin, and looks at it, like she's trying to solve a fuckin' mystery or somethin'.

"He's not on the napkin, sweetie. But call him, and tell him I referred you. And tell him, if he wants to take a walk on the wild side, to give me a call."

Shawn
There is a God

A consulting meeting with a new bank in central Jersey will take up most of my day today. Could mean big money if I get this account. God has blessed me exceedingly, with this investment banking business and consulting firm. Damn, I feel good as hell right now. Been in this hot shower for about twenty minutes so far, and I have no real plans to get out any time soon. Well, not until the hot water runs out. One thing I kept from Lee Lee's skank ass were her shower gels and lotions. Call me a bitch, that's fine, but I love the way this shit smells and feels when I'm in the shower. Smelling it makes me think of Aaliyah, yet, I don't miss her. This one is called sweet lavender, and I love it. The idea about the CD player in the bathroom was an original she tried to claim, but I know she got that idea from Amber, and it's a hot one. Music playing, combined with an intense shower makes it hard to leave the bathroom.

Usher's *Can You Handle It* is on repeat, for obvious reasons. It was the song playing when I made love to her, Amber that is. The song is hot as hell, and reminds me of her. Shit, I haven't been intimate with anyone since then, which is another reason for the whole hour-long showers and the smooth shower gels. I remember that day, like it was yesterday, and how my heart has stood frozen in time since then.

"I'm sure, Shawn." *She took me by the hand and led me into the bedroom.*

My heart raced. I heard Usher's Can You Handle It, *playing softly in the background. Not only had Amber put on music, but she's lit candles too. That's what she was doing when I heard her moving around in here.*

She stopped at the side of the bed and turned to face me. Her mouth devoured mine and our tongues become entangled. The passion, the heat, the connection...it's all so surreal. All of a sudden, I realized I'd never felt that way about any woman in my life! I wanted her so badly, but it's not just sexually. I wanted her wholeheartedly, her mind, her body, and her soul. I wanted Amber to be mine, to be my wife, to be the one I would love, honor and cherish all of my days. I picked her up and laid her on the bed.

For a while, I laid there with her while my hands hesitantly roamed all over her body. I needed to have her. She quivered and gyrated as my hands discovered and become acquainted with all that is good, and precious and dear. As I cradled her face in the palm of my hands, my tongue lost its way, deep in the abyss of her soul. She's no longer crying, and she seemed to be at peace.

My hands somehow found their way to her blouse. I began unbuttoning when she reached to help me, all the while staring into my eyes. Her skin felt flawless and silky smooth, her body, beautiful. She's absolutely perfect.

I got up from the bed and began taking off my clothes, still holding Amber in my gaze, while she tugged at me, trying to pull me closer to her, grabbing my hands, sucking my fingers, slowly caressing my chest with her fingertips, kissing my navel, licking my nipples. I was afraid if I lost eye contact with her, I'd wake up and it would have all been just a dream. I laid back down beside her.

I really don't have time for dating, and don't want to be bothered with women and their fucked up games. I was always up front with a chick. If I wanted something long-term, I made that clear. If not, I made that clear too. What Aaliyah did to me, put me on my heels, brought all my defenses up, and has made me more cautious than I was already. And what I experienced with Amber, was enough to fuck the strongest of men up. I thought I was strong, but that day, that one day, just totally fucked me up, mind, body and soul. Khalil had better realize he's a blessed man.

Damn, she's sexy. My lips found her mouth as I licked her lips again and again and her neck, and finally her breast where I playfully teased her nipples with my tongue, gently biting them, sucking them, kissing them, and loving them. Damn, she smelled so good. I felt myself ready to bust wide open. My hand caressed her body and moved between her things where the heat from her sweetness began to rise. I heard her let out the most tantalizing moan I'd ever heard. Damn! I was ready for her, but I also wanted to take my time. The thought that I'd probably never get this chance again made me want to do it right. I needed to stroke her pain away.

I wanted Amber to feel safe with me. I wanted to be her protector. I wanted to be the one who washed away her pain, her doubts, and her fears. I wanted to take her heart under my wing and be its guardian.

The warm light flickered from the candles dancing in her eyes. Another tear rolled down her cheek. I kissed it away. I looked deep into her eyes and placed her hand on my heart.

"Look at me Amber." I needed her to, not only hear what I had to say, but feel it as well.

She faintly responds, "Yes."

"You don't ever have to cry again, Amber, and I mean that shit from the bottom of my heart." More tears fell from her eyes. I, in turn, began crying all over again.

I kissed her all over her body and found my way down to her navel. She smelled so good; I wanted to smell her for the rest of my life. She trembled underneath me and released all kinds of moans, as if I was already inside her.

I was born a patient lover, so I began with her feet. Lifting her leg and placing her foot up to my face, I gently licked around her perfectly painted red toes. I kissed her feet, sucked her toes, and traveled down her thigh, with my tongue. Small baby kisses took me closer and closer to her magic. Becoming nearer to her wonderment had me in a state of bliss, a state of pure ecstasy. Finally, I get to where I wanted to be. She's so wet, drenched, tender and inviting, so soft, supple, moist, succulent and smelled so sweet. I tasted her. I'd eaten pussy before, but there was something different about that time. I want to be there. I needed to be there. I didn't tease her or play with it, as I'd done in the past, with other women.

I sucked Amber with my soul, like if I sucked her long enough, maybe her pain will dissipate. My tongue danced around inside her goodness in a way it never had before, with anyone. I held on to her thighs and loved her with my spirit. In and out, out and in, my tongue found every inch of her and had the audacity to introduce itself as her new comforter. Kissing her pussy lips, licked them slowly, and admired the juices that flowed uncontrollably, made everything inside me want to emerge to the surface. My heart, vulnerable and naked, was now on my sleeve. That woman, laying there with me...my best friend's wife...was all the woman I'd ever needed.

Her juices flowing, her legs trembled and her continuous sultry moans caused me to slow my pace. Some how I'd managed to escape into my own world, because I could no longer hear her sounds, her moans, and her pleasure. I slowly moved up to face her. She welcomed me back into her arms and kissed me softly.

"I love you, Shawn. Promise me that whatever happens, you'll never hurt me?"

I didn't have to think twice before answering her. "I already told you Amber. I promise you, for as long as I live....I got you, baby."

Her tears started again right along with mine. We cried in unison as our emotions got the best of us. It was deep and we both were fully aware of the magnitude of our encounter. All I could think of, at that moment, was keeping her safe. Keeping her with me.

Breathing had become so heavy and so erratic. The kissing, so carnal and passionate. Our tongues danced with the devil, as we couldn't hold on any longer. I slowly laid on top of her and parted her legs with mine. The anticipation of what was yet to come had made me solid as a rock.

Who the hell is it now? My damn phone ringing puts a cease order on my trip down memory fucking lane. I swear my phone rings day and night, night and day and is becoming a bit overwhelming. Aaliyah calls three to ten times a fucking day, with the same shit, and it drives me crazy. This better not be her, interrupting me from my sweet shower.

Stepping out of the bathroom, I leave the shower on, and walk into the kitchen, butt naked, to retrieve my phone. I like to leave it on the charger as I'm getting dressed in the mornings, this way I am guaranteed a full charge. With my busy days, I need my phone at its peak.

"Whoa!" I yell as I enter the kitchen, trying to maintain my balance. I almost bust my ass, slipping on the damn floor. That's what I get for walking out here dripping wet. Reaching for the phone, I catch it on the last ring, before it went into voicemail.

"Hello?" I ask, as I lean on the kitchen counter.

"Hi, Mr. Fontaine," a sweet, sexy voice greets me on the other end.

"Yes, this is Shawn Fontaine." I adjust my tone to sound ultra-professional. I throw in a little Barry White for good measure.

"Hi, I'm sorry to call so early. Is this a good time?"

"Sure, as long as this is not a telemarketer."

"Ha, ha, ha. No, I'm not a telemarketer."

Damn, she sounds very sexy, whoever she is. And I can't believe I even noticed. "Well, if I may ask, who's calling?"

"My name is Summer. I was referred to you by Scott LaBelle. He gave me your number because I would like to start investing my money. He said you were the best."

Well how about that? Scott's punk ass is good for something after all. But LaBelle? He assumed that name a few years back. I guess it goes with his whole stylist image. Leave it to Scott to have the last name of LaBelle. I want to laugh out loud, but I can't, considering this is a professional call. I walk my naked ass into my living room, and retrieve my briefcase, pull out the notepad to take down all of Summer's information. Nice name, I think to myself. Nice voice too.

"Oh yes, I know Scott, for years now. I'll have to thank him the next time we speak. So Summer, how can I help you?"

"Thank you, Mr. Fontaine, I…"

I cut her off. "Listen, Summer. Any friend of Scott is a friend of mine. Call me Shawn. It's cool."

"Okay, Shawn. I need help balancing my money. And since I've gotten a serious promotion, along with my master's degree, I'm making more money. And to be blunt, before I go out there and spend it on frivolous things, I think the best thing to do is to invest."

"Smart move, Summer."

"Thanks, Shawn."

"Okay, this is what I want for you to do."

"I'm listening, Shawn."

"By the way, you have a beautiful speaking voice, Summer."

"Thanks, Shawn. I was just thinking that you sound so handsome on the phone. Not to flirt or anything, it's just a compliment."

"I hear you. So, this is what I want for you to do. Go to my web site. It's www dot Shawn Fontaine dot investments dot com."

"Okay, I will go right now, since I'm online."

"Great," I say to her, thinking that this girl has got her shit in order. It's impressive, considering what I've witnessed in the recent past.

"Oh my," she chuckles softly.

"Are you there?" I ask, wondering why she made the "oh my" comment.

"Yes, I'm here, Mr. Fontaine, I mean, Shawn."

"Good."

"You're very handsome. I see why Scott said what he did."

"Thank you. But what did Scott say?" I ask, but not really sure I want to know the answer.

"Ha, ha. He said that if you're ready to take a walk on the wild side, to give him a call." Summer laughs a soft, sexy laugh. Damn, mami sounds good as hell on this phone. Probably looks like road kill though. That would be just my luck.

"I was scared to ask what Scott said. I see why now," I say to her, laughing along with her.

"Did I tell you that you have a beautiful voice, Summer?"

"Yes, you did, Shawn. And thank you."

"I'm sorry, I don't mean to be rude."

"It's okay, Shawn."

"Okay, your voice has me in a trance. I forgot what I was telling you to do."

"Ha, that's cute. You were telling me to go to your web site, and I did that, and saw your handsome profile."

"Ha, yes, I remember now. Glad you like what you see…"

She cuts me off. "I do like what I see, Shawn," she responds, sounding good as shit, so much so, that my dick gets a little longer. Yep, it is, as I see it growing right before my eyes.

"Thank you, Summer. By the way, is that your real name?"

"Yes, my name is Summer Rain Kelly."

"That's a beautiful name. What do you do for a living?"

"I work for immigration. In the detainment and deporting division. I head the division now, actually."

"Oh shit, now! Congrats, sister. Oh, are you a sister?" I ask, hoping I haven't crossed the line. "I don't mean to offend you."

"Yes, I am. I'm a sister, Shawn. A thirty-two year old, professional black woman, single, no children," she tells me throwing hints so big they bitch slap me in the forehead.

"Is that right?"

"Yep."

Well, Summer Rain, you sound like you got it going on."

"Thank you, Shawn."

"Okay, so complete the online form there on my site. I'll upload the information into my laptop after I put on some clothes. You caught me right out of the shower."

"Wow!"

"Wow, what?" I ask, confused by her last statement.

"Yes, wow. But I'll reserve my comments," she slightly chuckles in a sort of sexy kind of way.

My dick is on the rise. I've never been on the phone with a woman whom I've never met, and had such a visceral reaction. "Okay, but I expect you to tell me at some point."

"I hope I get the opportunity to, Mr. Fontaine."

"What's your number, Summer? I want to program it into my phone."

"Please do. It's 555-215-2980. Call me anytime."

"I will. Make sure you complete that application and profile information. I will check it as soon as I'm done with my shower."

"Oh, I'm sorry. Did I interrupt your shower?"

"Yes, but that's okay. The water is still running, and as long as it's hot, I won't charge you for your time," I laugh out loud.

"I'm sure it's still hot, Shawn."

Okay, honey dip is cute, and now my shit is on swole. "Have a good day, Summer."

"You too, Shawn. And thanks for your time."

"Anytime," I respond, still looking at my chocolate bar.

After hanging up the phone, I run back into the bathroom, but this time, the wetness of the floor, catches up with me, and I bust my ass, right before reaching the shower. I laugh out loud, as I pick myself up off of the floor, and get back to my shower.

My mind floats back to that forbidden land, restricted place, where I got back to my bedroom on that both magical and dreaded day and Amber resurfaces.

"Shawn?"

I know what she's about to ask me. Protection. I reached over and opened the nightstand drawer, without even answering her.

"No, Shawn. I want to feel you."

"Amber, baby, I need to feel you too."

I hesitated for a moment and then kissed her softly. I noticed that more tears were formed in her eyes. They had not yet fallen. I maneuvered my manhood directly atop her warmth. I grind on her, teasing her until she moaned, and I lost my tongue in her mouth, once again. Her lips were so sweet. She kissed me back with such dedication, so much passion.

I couldn't take it any longer. With one thrust, I was inside of her. I cried out. She cried out. She's so tight, so wet, and so hot. I can't believe I was inside of Amber. I could see her nipples getting harder right before my eyes. Her body shuddered.

An unfamiliar feeling ran through my being. It's not just the sex but the totality of all that wais inside of me. I held her tight, as I, somehow, climbed higher. Somehow dug deeper. She's so wet and so soft that I felt her walls of comfort give way to each of my blows. Our solaced spirits amiss earth-shaking harmony as I rise to depths unbeknownst to mankind. I'd had sex plenty of times but I realized then that it was the first time I'd ever truly made love.

"Amber, I love you." I managed to say those four little words before our historical encounter almost ended. I felt the spasms begin, but I didn't want it to end. Not yet. Oh God, that feeling. That spiritual magic that had been absent from my life for so long. Suddenly I heard her calling out to me.

"Shawn, I'm cummin'!"

Her warmth turned to heat. Her wetness drowned me so good. She had her legs wrapped around me so tight pulling me *in deeper and deeper. I took her mouth into mine, as if on cue and with so much determination.*

Unfeigned love empowered me as I stroked her with every inch of my body. Powerful, blunt forced impacts took me to deeper plains. Making love to her face-to–face, mouth-to-mouth, soul-to-soul became too much for me.

Amber's so sexy and sweet that I felt myself spiraling into a cosmic free-fall of intoxication. My head was spinning, and the air in the room seemed thin. Sweat ran down my head and I was dizzy. My body jerked. I tried to pull out. I couldn't. I wouldn't.

I slowed down with my thrusts and my strokes. I just wanted to rest in all her deliciousness. I would have loved for that to have gone on for hours. I needed to be inside of Amber for as long as I could. Nothing else in my life made sense anymore, aside from me loving her, making love to her and giving her all the love that she deserved, for so long. I pulled out slowly so I wouldn't explode. She grabbed me.

"Shawn, please. It's okay."

I placed a single finger over her lips as I got up from the bed. "Shhhhh, It's not over baby, I promise."

I moved from the bed while holding Amber in my gaze. Her eyes followed my every move. She's so sweet and looked so fragile. I want to take my time with her. Go slow, be gentle.

I told her to turn to her side; instead, she crawled on her knees to the edge of the bed where I stood. She took me into her hand and placed me into her mouth. She took me all in with those full, wet lips and went down the shaft with her tongue. That felt so good, but she's going to make me cum with quickness, and I can't let it end like this. I tried to tell her to stop, but I couldn't get it out. I ran my fingers through her hair. I admired her body—those full breasts and fat ass, as she sucked me down so good.

I couldn't take that anymore, not then; I needed to be inside of her again. "Amber, turn to your side."

I slowly pulled out of her mouth, wishing like hell, I could hold on longer. She obliged. Her silhouette wavered in the background, overshadowed by the flames from the candles. The sight of her from the rear made my heart race faster. I got back into the bed with her. I spooned her from behind and held her as tight as I could.

Her warm body, her soft skin, her smell even made me feel like I'd died and gone to Heaven. That was the shit I'd been missing out on all my life. True love in its most deep and purest form. I leaned in and gently nibbled on her ear, licking it softly. The urge to reassure her that I loved her compelled me.

"Amber, I love you." My tongue slid down her neck. "Are you okay?"

She turned her head slightly and responded, "Yes baby."

Her body trembled in my arms, and my manhood swelled as I massaged it against her ass. I knew she wanted me, and I wanted to give it to her with all that I had. Still behind her, I lifted her voluptuous leg with one arm. She leaned back and rested her head on my shoulder.

I inserted deeply, with conviction, and her drenched core grabbed hold of me. We both cried out in unison as our bodies combined once more. I felt how soaked she was and I know its going to be hard for me to hold on, but I can't let this go.

My hands took on a mind of their own as I caressed her body, her breasts, and her thighs. With one hand, I reached around her and teasingly fondled her clit as I delivered, even more, powerful thrusts. I was loving her, as if I'd been loving her for years.

Amber moaned and quivered as I moved in and out of her. I pulled all the way out and then ease back in, over and over again. The sensation her pussy left on my shaft was indescribable, its so good. Her drenched core had a hold of me, and I couldn't hold on any longer. With desperation, I whispered in her ear.

"Tell me you love me, Amber."

"Oh God Shawn...I think I've always loved you."

I go deeper and deeper as we both made noises that could awaken the dead. She reached back and grabbed my ass to pull me further into her righteousness. I'm in love with this woman. Wholeheartedly. Concretely. And at that very moment, I called out her name as I emptied myself inside of her. And I know, from that point on...Amber was mine.

So glad that I'm able to move forward. Took me a minute, but I have moved on. As long as I don't see her, I'm good. Reality definitely set in when she decided to remain with her husband. Another fifteen minutes have passed, and the water is finally cold. As I make my way out of the bathroom, in towel only, I head over to my laptop to see if Summer has uploaded her information. She has. I'm impressed. Not a high income to debt ratio, which means I can really help her. I love to see our black women succeeding and becoming more financially savvy. Well, would you look at this. She even sent a picture of her and Scott, with a note attached: *Thanks for your time. All the best, Summer.*

Aw, she's sweet. And look at her. She's fine too. Butter-rich skin, which seems to be smooth and silky. These pictures can fuck you up sometimes. Long, jet black hair. And look at them tits. Damn. She's right up my alley. She's about an inch or two shorter than Scott's flaming gay ass, which means she's about five-nine. Nice and thick too, just like I like them. Damn, what am I saying? Let me fall back. I'm sounding like a child. Child or not, I see them pretty light-skinned legs, and thick thighs.

As my body dries, I grab the cocoa butter, and begin applying it to smooth this rough, ashy exterior. I can't seem to get Summer's voice out of my mind. Honey dip got it going on. I decide to call her back to confirm receipt of her information.

Picking up my phone to dial her, my phone rings before I can do so. The caller ID registers as a blocked number and I am hesitant to answer, but I need to. Shit, it may be the next big deal.

"Good morning. Shawn Fontaine speaking."

"Shawn?"

Oh, Lord.

"Yes?"

"Baby, can we talk for a minute."

"No, Aaliyah. We can't. About what?"

"About me and you, Shawn," Aaliyah manages to say in between sniffles.

"Aaliyah. It's first thing in the morning. A weekday morning at that. I'm getting ready for work."

"Can you give me five minutes, Shawn."

"Hurry up. I'll put you on speaker while I get dressed."

"Okay."

"Speak, Aaliyah."

"Wait Shawn. You're not dressed?"

"Not yet."

"I miss you, Shawn. I miss your touch, your feel. I miss you, baby."

"I'm sure you do, Aaliyah," I blush. I know she misses me. But I can't go back down that beaten path.

"Shawn, don't you miss touching me? Kissing me? I know you do."

"I did miss you for a minute, Aaliyah, of course, I loved you at one point."

"Loved me? You don't love me anymore, Shawn?" Aaliyah screams.

"Not anymore, Aaliyah."

"How can you just throw our love away so easily, Shawn?"

"I hope you're looking in the mirror while you're asking me that, Aaliyah. The real question is. How could you throw it all away? I loved you, Aaliyah, and I was here for you, ready to make you my wife. I've never asked any other woman to be my wife. You threw that all away."

"But I'm sorry, Shawn!" Aaliyah cries uncontrollably.

And just when I thought this conversation couldn't get any more weird, the devil herself, gets on the line.

"Shawn, you need to stop fuckin' playin'. Nigga, you know you want her back!" Shayla's stinking, skank ass gets on the line and yells.

"Shayla, get your nasty, ho, triflin' ass off my phone!"

"Nigga, who you calling nasty?"

"I'm calling you nasty, Shayla. Now, put Aaliyah back on the…"

"Back on the what, nigga?"

"Oh, never mind. Y'all two chickenheads have a good life."

After hanging up the phone on Amos and Andy, Laverne and Shirley, Dumb and Dumber, I throw on my checked boxer briefs, and white wife beater, my dark green dress socks and reach for my slacks in the closet. Going with the olive green Brooks Brothers suit today, with yellow button up and striped tie. I got my Stacy Adams gators on. *Damn*, I think to myself as I stand in front of my full-length mirror, well, actually, its Aaliyah's but, oh well. I look pretty damn good today.

All is packed into my briefcase and the phone is fully charged. I head to the kitchen to grab a glass of OJ, and remember that I want to call Summer back. Love that name, Summer. Reaching for my phone, I look at the notepad, and see her number and decide to give her a call.

"Good morning." Her voice sounds sweet. Damn, I could listen to that voice for hours.

"Good morning, again," I smile, as I pack the rest of my shit into my briefcase.

"Yes it is a good morning."

There is a brief silence on the line.

"May I ask who's calling?"

"This is the boogeyman," I chuckle.

"I'm unafraid of the boogeyman."

"Is that right?"

"Yes. I actually like horror films." She laughs a soft and sensual chuckle.

"Well, if you like horror films, you should see me in the morning," I laugh, while putting on the alarm to my loft.

"That doesn't sound like horror to me. Sounds like a privilege. Okay, I'm sorry. That was definitely flirting, Mr. Fontaine, and I have to apologize. I'm normally not so forward and blunt. But you're very approachable. Hope I didn't offend you."

"No need to apologize. Like I said, any friend of Scott is a friend of mine. I know its all in fun. So listen, I did receive your information and I believe that I can help you out. It would be my pleasure. Give me a year, and I will double your investments."

"That sounds good, Shawn. I'm so hyped!"

"And thanks for the photo of you and Scott. It's really nice."

"Yes, I figured I'd put a face to the name."

"Well, you definitely did that. You're a beautiful woman."

"Thank you, Shawn. I appreciate that."

"Anytime. Ha, ha, ha."

"Why are you laughing, Shawn?"

"I'm laughing because I hardly know you, and I've taken you from my shower, to my kitchen to my car and now, I'm on the road, actually heading toward the Lincoln Tunnel."

"Well, I feel honored, Shawn. Meetings today?"

"Yes ma'am. Two huge meetings today that could be really good for my business."

"I know you're dressed to impress."

"Thanks Summer. Nothing big, just an olive green business suit."

She sighs, and replies, "Mmm. Sounds good. How tall are you?"

"I'm about six-foot-three, and you?"

"I'm five-nine, Shawn."

"Nice."

More silence speaks to both of us through the receivers and I take the opportunity to put on some good music. I'm in the mood for some grown and sexy music, so I pop in the O'Jays greatest hits CD. My momz played them all of my life, so I know every song. This is what I call real music, not some watered-down soul music. This is the real shit. I begin to sing out loud. "Said we cried, cried, cried, we cried together...and then we, and then we, made love."

"Nice voice. I love the O'Jays."

"Thanks, dear. I love them too."

"So, listen, Summer. I could talk to you for hours, but I won't hold you. I have about an hour drive."

"I don't mind if you hold me, Shawn. Oops, I'm crossing that line again, huh?"

"It's all good, Summer. We just clicked, I suppose."

"Scott said you were a winner."

"Well, what do you think? Oh, tell Scott I said 'Thank you.'"

"I think you are a winner, for sure, Shawn."

Wow, this chick is saying all the right shit, along with looking and sounding the right way. There is a God, somewhere.

Keisha
Mahogany Punany

I ain't got time for this bullshit today. Up in here with these old ass muthafuckas, when I could be getting my damn feet and nails done. I'm hungry as shit, too. All I had for breakfast was two extra strength Tylenols, and some flat ass Pepsi. And I know better. My period is on, got me nasty and flowin' like the damn Hudson River; overflowed. I feel like shit, probably smell like shit, and don't wanna be bothered by shit. Well, I betta get ready for an interesting day, full of pad changes, bed pans, pill passing, and yes, Mrs. Sampson, my new patient.

This old bitch was just admitted here a few weeks ago and done already got on my goddamn nerves. Comin' in here actin' all high sadity, and shit. Amber actually spoke to the family, prior to her admission, and consoled her children, who didn't want to put her in a home. Most families don't and I don't blame them. But shit, after they come here, we take good care of them. Somethin' is definitely up with this bitch, though. I think she used to be an alcoholic back in the day, always with a damn bottle and cup next to her. Her mind done left her somethin' terrible. Her old ass don't realize she just drinkin' juice. Fuckin' apple juice.

Now, here I am, early as hell in the morning, fillin' in for one of these triflin' ass, young ass nurses who called out, on my fuckin' day off, and gotta deal with her old, itchy ass. She don't like me either and I don't care. After Amber admitted her, she naturally gravitated to Amber, being that my best friend is so fuckin' lily white. Now, all she want is Amber. When I have to take care of her, she shits on herself, pours fuckin' juice in the bed and does some real spiteful shit when I come around. I'm gonna teach her wrinkled ass a lesson too. Next time she wanna play the shit-on-yourself game, she gonna also play the sit-and-spin-in-your-own-shit game. She don't know? She betta ask somebody.

I walk into the bathroom on the fourth floor. Today I am working four main, then will go down to two main, which I nicknamed Haiti for all the Haitian nurses working on that floor. They 'bout black as me, but ain't nowhere near as fly as I am. I tell them flowery bitches, when you are dark, or big, or fat, or anything other than what this world tells us is beautiful, that you gotta rock that shit right, every time you leave your front door. My ass could compete with any bitch on the catwalk; try to touch me. They don't get it yet, but they will. We gotta reinvent our own images of beauty and make the world accept it. My black ass is sexy as shit, and muthafuckas betta recognize. I tell that to my big girls, to my fat girls, to my girls with short, nappy, taco-meat hair, to my skinny, shaped-like-a-boy girls too. All of us.

After changing my nasty ass for the third time this morning, I wash my hands, and adjust my nurse's scrubs. I wore the burgundy ones today to match the color of my period, just in case it wanted to make an impromptu appearance. If I had kids by now, I would schedule a hysterectomy for sometime next week. I'm a mean, evil bitch this time of the month. And everyone knows it.

Opening the door to the bathroom, leads me to the fourth floor nurses station. It's pretty quiet today. Checking my chart to see who's next on my rounds, confirms my disgust, as I am up next with a personal visit to see Mrs. Sampson again. Switching my ass off, I rock my hips hard as hell as I approach Mrs. Sampson's room, 'cause I know that new doctor, Dr. Peshine is watching me. He's scoping and jocking. A new doctor to the home; white as the driven snow, itching for a scratch and dying to catch the fever. Jungle fever. Yeah, he plays that shit off, but I know a curious cracker when I see one. He would give up a Porsche to have some mahogany punany hiding in his closet. He probably listen to N.W.A. or Public Enemy while he ridin' home to his gated community. Here he comes now.

Turning to my side, flicking my hair in a sexy ass move, I greet Dr. Cracker, I mean Dr. Peshine with a smile, and turn on my Wall Street, professional side. "Well, good morning, Dr. Peshine. How are you this lovely morning?"

Dr. Peshine, in blue scrubs, to match his blue eyes, runs his fingers through his jet-black hair, propping his hand on his hip, and smiles. Is that some sexy white boy shit? "I'm doing super, Keisha. Thanks for asking." He smiles more, and raises his eyebrow. Is that a come on? He gotsta come on better than that. Raising that one ass eyebrow ain't told me shit, other than he can impersonate The Rock. How 'bout pulling out a big ass black man dick? Now, that shit would impress the fuck outta me. "Are you headed to Mrs. Sampson's room?" he asks me, still sportin' that dumb ass Justin Timberlake grin.

I lick my lips, just to fuck with him a bit, placing my hand on my hips, and respond accordingly. "Yes, I am. How did you guess? I swear you are one of the smartest doctors at Divine Intervention!" I reach up to his six-foot-two frame, and pat him on his shoulder. I tell you, for a white boy, he ain't that bad, with them white ass Tom Cruise teeth.

Dr. Peshine follows me into Mrs. Sampson's room, and we find Mrs. Sampson watching television, and passing gas. This bitch got a damn song going on in here, fartin' like a fat man. I walk over to her, with her pretty ass, and pat her on the head.

"Good morning, Mrs. Sampson. How are you feeling?" I ask and crack the window just a bit to get rid of the two-week-old cabbage smell.

She looks at me and cracks a smile. "I'm alright."

Leave it to Beaver jumps in as he walks over to Mrs. Sampson. "So, no pains today?"

"Yes, doctor, I'm doing just fine."

Dr. Peshine examines Mrs. Sampson, as I stand on the sidelines. Once he's done, I take her into the bathroom, and bathe her stinkin' ass, lotion her down, and sit her into the loungin' chair. "Mrs. Sampson, you sit here, and I will have your linens changed for you. You want to get back into a nice, fresh bed, right?" I say to her as I lean in and give her a sweet smile.

"Okay, Mrs. Sampson, I will check in on you later. Keisha, please come by my office once you're done," Dr. Peshine tells me as he leaves the room.

"Got to hell."

I could've sworn I heard something. Putting on Mrs. Sampson's slippers, after replacing her socks, I hear it again.

"Go to hell, you black bitch."

I know I done heard wrong. But just to be sure, I look up at Mrs. Sampson, who now looks like Linda Blair in *The Exorcist*, all frightenin' and shit. Looked like she done transformed into Satan in old lady form.

"Mrs. Sampson, did you say something to me?"

"Yeah."

"Oh, what did you say?"

"I said, go to hell, you black bitch."

I laugh out loud, 'cause this bitch don't know how close she is to going out the damn window, face first. "Now, that's not nice, Mrs. Sampson." I hand her a glass of orange juice.

"Shut up."

"Now, you weren't this mean when Dr. Peshine was here, now were you?"

She smiles a real vindictive, yellow-tooth smile at me. What is it with me and these patients?

"Dr. Peshine is nice. You, now you, you just look like a slave."

She didn't just call me a damn slave? So I ask her to repeat that shit for good measure. "What was that, Mrs. Sampson?"

"I said, you blacky, yo' black ass look like a negro slave. Straight out of the motherland." Mrs. Sampson laughs out loud, like Oprah Winfrey in *The Color Purple*, when they were all at the dinner table. All demented and shit.

To prevent myself from fuckin' this old lady up, I summon the nurse's aid to finish changing her linens and put her back in bed. But before doing so, I whisper into Mrs. Sampson's darling little wax-filled ear, "You betta watch your back, bitch."

For the life of me, I can't possibly understand why Dr. Peshine wants for me to come to his office. I may be a ghetto-ass bitch from time to time, but I'm a good nurse. Walking towards his office, I finally reach his door, and tap on it slightly before opening it. I see Dr. Peshine sitting at his cherry wood finished desk, and he smiles that Brady Bunch smile for me once more.

"Have a seat Keisha," he points to the high-back leather chair, "I wanted to talk with you."

I sit my ass down, and I could use the rest. My ass is hurting, as well as my feet, and my cramps are kicking into overdrive. "Yes, Dr. Peshine? Is everything okay?"

"Yes, Keisha." He gets up from his desk and walks over to me. "All is well, but please call me Greg. My name is Gregory Peshine."

"Okay, Greg." I look up at him. "Is all well?"

Greg takes the seat next to me. "Keisha, I've never done this before and I hope I don't come across as unprofessional. But, I was wondering if we could do dinner one evening after work, or maybe even on a weekend."

I smile, and as black as I am, I swear I'm blushing. "Well, Greg, I'm flattered, but I'm casually dating someone right now."

"So, casually means not serious, right?"

"Right. He's a friend of a friend, nothing too serious."

"Well, that's good to know. Because Keisha," taking my hand into his, "you are one of the most sexy women I've ever seen in my life."

"Is that right?"

"Absolutely. You are gorgeous and I would love to get to know you better."

"Okay, Greg, where are the hidden cameras?"

"This is not a joke. I talked to Amber, and she told me that you were very approachable, so I wanted to try my luck."

Amber's ass is gonna pay. I guess her high-yellow ass don't want to be the only one in the middle of a fuckin' love triangle.

"Did she?"

"Yes. I told her how I felt about you."

"Well, okay, Greg. Let's see how things go with my current friend. I guess I could make some time to do dinner with you."

"You won't be disappointed, Keisha."

"I'm sure I won't."

I head out of Greg's office, feeling awkward as hell, 'cause I know he's looking at my booty. After I close the door to his office, I face the nurse's station again, and see just the person I want to talk to. She's smiling from ear to ear, and walks over toward me.

"Hey, Keisha." She hugs me, and kisses me on the cheek.

I politely grab her arm and drag her ass down the hall. "Amber, what the hell were you thinking, telling Greg to come and talk to me?"

"Who's Greg?"

"Dr. Peshine, goddamnit!"

She blushes and covers her mouth, and starts to do her little happy dance, which Khalil and Shawn may think is adorable, but it makes me sick.

"He's a cutie, right, Keisha?" She gives me another hug.

"Amber!"

"Well, Keisha?"

I break down. "Yeah, girl, he is cute as hell, with them damn blue eyes. But you know I'm dating Jamal."

A look of disgust crosses her face. "You are not dating Jamal. You are wasting time. I hope you ain't give him no ass."

"No, Amber, as a matter of fact, I ain't give him none."

"Good."

"And how is that good?"

"Because you'll be dating Greg soon, and will slowly get rid of Jamal."

"Uh huh."

"Trust me, Keisha. I know these things."

"Yeah, just like you know who you in love with, right?"

Amber looks at me like she just lost her mother..

"Speaking of which, Keisha, you're still coming with me, right?"

"To the doctor?"

"Yeah."

"Wouldn't miss it for the world, sister."

Summer
Dream Weaver

The residue of his jism still lingers in my mouth, in the corners even, on my tongue, on my fingertips. The after taste of it is bitter sweet, sort of like drinking cranberry juice; the taste survives way after the juice is gone. But you know what you've just swallowed is good for you. He made my pussy so wet, so hot; it was throbbing, yearning just for a taste of him. My legs were dying, begging to part just to feel him deep inside me. I'd been fucked a few times before, but this time, this beautiful Black creature with me tonight, made me cum for no reason at all. I was happy to down his juice, drink his babies, swirl my tongue in it. He is supreme and for that reason, I'll basically do anything this man asks. I wanted to drink all he poured down my throat, but there was no more left. I sucked him dry. No, I didn't mind, not at all. I'd give up a paycheck to keep him near. I'd sell my soul just to stay in his bed. That's real shit right there. And this is just round number one.

I insisted on sucking his dick first. In any new situation, usually both people are so excited that premature cummin' is bound to happen. I knew if I let him rub one out with a quickness, he'd have some real stroke-ability for round two. No problem baby, this one is on me I told myself. I was right.

Round two came and it was on and poppin' for real. He stroked me so good, real deep like he was digging for gold. I must've yelled out all kinds of expletives, and probably even cursed his parents out, because the shit was so damn good. Dick was so delightful; I wanted to write a check right then and there. I have to remember to thank his mother for giving birth to him. He's a talented brother and deserved the Oscar for best performance by a pussylover. I say "Gotdamn!"

I remember how it began. We met for dinner at Chateau of Spain, a nice Spanish restaurant right in the heart of downtown Newark. Not aesthetically competing with many of the fine restaurants in the Bricks, but the food made up for what it lacked in visual appeal.

Although I'd been in his presence briefly, there was nothing that could prepare me for all the deliciousness that I encountered. He was grand.

I told him what I'd be wearing that evening. Nothing special—a silver halter with belt to match and some white gauchos. I wanted to be sexy and cute but not over the top. We women tend to over do it when it comes to getting the attention and affection of the opposite sex. I figured our conversation over the weeks had pulled him in closer to me, so I had a running start to his heart. If he didn't like me in the flesh, then oh well, we had a decent friendship so I was not too worried. What the hell am I talking about? I'm scared as hell right now!

"Would you like another, Miss?" asks the bartender, a little Spanish man, who takes away my glass of White Zinfandel.

"No, thank you. I'm just waiting for my date to arrive." He comes back a few seconds later with a Brandy Alexander. I push the drink back toward him. "No thanks. I didn't want anything else." I'm trying to be polite.

"This is your favorite drink, right?" The voice alone sends a quiver through my entire being. I'm nervous, frightened, shook, elated, all at the same time. Please don't let this be another broke as nigga.

I exhale, push my shoulders back and turn around in my bar stool and witness the miracle of God himself as I look into his beautiful brown eyes. They're even more dreamy in person, up close and personal, not behind the corporate attire. Oh God, I've never done this before, but I'm as happy as a pig in shit right now. I put on the happiest, sexiest smile that I'd been practicing all day in the mirror and I am one hundred percent sure that it is a charming one, as he smiles too.

"Summer?"

"Yes, I'm Summer."

He smiles, bends down, kisses me respectfully on my cheek. Wow, he smells divine. I have to remind myself after I fuck him, of course, to ask him what cologne he's wearing.

He pulls back away from my face, eyes steadily looking me up and down, and his lips part with the sexiest grin to a mouth of perfectly straight, white teeth. His smile alone makes me want to sit on his face.

"I'm Shawn. Shawn Fontaine. Nice to *finally* meet you."

I get up out of my bar stool and give him a big hug. Damn, he feels so good, so strong, like a stallion. Ooh, he's so tall, so dark, and so scrumptious. He places his well-defined arms around me and embraces me with dedication, like he wants me to feel safe in his arms. My titties feel so good on his chest. And he's so tall, so fine, and so divine; I want to make him mine. Okay, okay that's corny, but you get the point. He has to be about six-feet-two. And I love it. Oh God, I love him already. I pull back to let him breathe but I don't want to let go.

We both smile and look at each other with sinful intentions, well at least on my part. I'm no slut, but I really want to fuck the shit out of him right now. He looks so good in his checkered button up shirt and gray slacks. Ooh, look at those feet! Yes, honey, it's gonna be on tonight!

I can't help but to remember our many conversations. We've been talking for so many weeks now that I know almost everything about him. Although we began communicating on a purely professional basis, thanks to Scott, I know about his bad breakup with his ex-fiancé, Aaliyah. I even know about his friendship with his best friend Khalil and the affection he has for Khalil's wife, Amber. He said they are all the best of friends. I know one thing; I'd better not catch up with Aaliyah, ever, for how dirty she did him. Look at his gorgeous black ass. How could she? Well, to each his own. But I'll tell you one thing, right here, right now. If I get the chance to love this supreme being right here, I'll never let him go. Come hell or high water, this man will be mine.

"Summer, if you don't mind, I'd rather go someplace quiet where we can talk. Get to know one another a little better. Cool?"

"Sure, Shawn. What do you have in mind?"

"Let me ride you over to my place in the city. It's only twenty minutes away. I promise I won't hurt you."

He didn't just say let me ride you? Shit you can ride me 'til Kingdom come. "That sounds good, Shawn. But aren't you hungry? Why don't we get you some dinner first?"

"I definitely plan on eating, Summer, once we get back to my place."

Shit, damn, motherfucker. Oh Lord! Okay. Calm down. I regain my composure, not that he can see that it was ever lost, and take his hand. "Sounds good, Shawn. I'm so glad we are finally getting some time in together."

"Me too, Summer. Me too."

Shawn leads the walk to his car from the restaurant. We're hand in hand, but I slightly trail behind him, and yes, I am looking at his ass. Big long, muscular legs, and juicy booty he has makes for a beautiful view. I think he can feel me staring at his ass as he turns around and smiles. "You look beautiful, Summer."

"Thank you, Shawn. I try."

"Well, you don't have to put forth much effort."

Okay, okay, that's it, we fucking!

After a smooth, evening ride into the city, while chillin' to the tight sounds of Gnarls Barkley, we finally arrive.

Shawn opens the door to his loft in the city and lets me in. It's gorgeous in here. "Shawn, this is really beautiful. You have great taste."

I walk in deeper into the living area. He's trailing behind me but not too far. I turn around to greet him with my smile of approval. He's staring at me. Moving in closer, he drops his keys on the coffee table. "Are you going to show me around?"

Shawn comes in even more close, grabs my titties and massages the nipples with his thumbs, through my halter. I don't know why, but I don't even try to stop him.

"Shawn, what are you doing?" I say with a look of sheer pleasure.

"Exactly what you want me to do, Summer."

I couldn't deny it either. We've shared so much for so long it seems I am very comfortable with him. Each time he rubs my nipples, my clit throbs. I'm wet, so wet right now, but scared of what to do. I don't want him to think I'm a ho, but I want to be *his* whore so fucking bad. Shawn takes his hands, reaches in towards my face with his left hand, takes his thumb and opens my mouth. Parting my lips slowly, as he looks at me, almost through me. He licks my bottom lip, then my top lip, then lets his tongue play with mine, without giving it all to me.

"Let me taste you, baby. I've been waiting so long to taste you."

I think I just came all over myself. I start to rub his nipples back, slowly unbuttoning his shirt, loosening his belt, his pants fall to the floor, he steps out of them, kisses me passionately, giving me the tongue over and over again, slowly, patiently. He takes off his shirt. Takes me over to the couch and begins to undress me. I stop him. I have to suck his dick. I take it out of his white, Calvin Klein boxer briefs. What a sight to behold. Big, fat, juicy, chocolate dick pointed straight ahead at me, screaming, "suck me." So I oblige. I suck that dick like my life depends on it. Sucking it like a champ, lovely swirls and licks, deep-throat it until he explodes. He tries to be a gentleman and pull it out, but I grab his ass cheeks and push him back into my mouth. I want him to release there.

"Summer! Summer! You have a call on line one." The sound of Crystal's voice breaks me from the most tantalizing daydream I've ever had. "Thank you, Crystal. Close the door on your way out, please."

I pick up the phone. "This is Summer, can I help you?"

"Hi Miss Summer Rain Kelly. How are you today? It's your favorite banker, Shawn. Shawn Fontaine."

"Well hello, Shawn. I was just thinking about you."

Amber
Too Close for Comfort

Reaching toward the dash to call Scott from my cell, I press three, and his phone rings. Keisha and I are riding along; listening to an old R. Kelly classic CD, *12 Play*, and on our way to Scott's to pick him up. I still don't completely understand why both Scott and Keisha insist on coming to the doctor with me, but it's easier to allow them to come, rather than try to dissuade them.

"Hello, Scott?"

"Nigga, did you see that shit? See, whoever produced this movie ain't have their facts straight. Oh…um…Amber, is that you, baby girl?"

"Yes, it's me, Scott."

"I'm sorry, sweetie. I'm sitting here watching *Transporter 2*, with Dexter St. Jock. Ha ha, excuse me. Well, you don't know him. Any who, baby girl, this movie is so fuckin' ridiculous. Amber, this bitch done put up two guns in front of two cops and she's still alive! Let that be a black man, and let his ass have the audacity to hold up two wallets, and see what happens to him in thirty seconds!"

I'm bent over laughing, as so is Keisha, as Scott confesses, while on speakerphone.

Undeniably hearing our laughter, Scott retorts. "Y'all

bitches know I'm right! Where are you, Amber?"

"I'm about ten minutes away. So be ready. And no, we're not riding in your car, and no, I don't have the pickup, I have Khalil's Escalade."

"Is that right? So, we'll be riding in style today I take it. Good, because like I always say; I'll never be caught dead in a busted ride, honey, trust!"

"Okay, Scott. We'll see you in a minute, crazy man!"

Of course, Keisha has to throw her forty-two cents in. "Don't you mean crazy fag, Amber?"

"I heard that, Miss Jane Pittman. I'll see you in a minute, Miss Celie!"

Keisha can't resist, and throws in the last word for good measure. "Bye, you twinkle toes." I press the button to clear the line from Scott. Keisha continues. "Amber, I don't know how you continue to deal with that faggot." Keisha and I give each other a quick glance, and burst out into uncontrollable laughter.

"Believe it or not, Keisha, I love that fag to death. Same way I love you."

Pulling up to Scott's driveway makes me reminiscent of our childhood. Scott didn't grow up under the best of circumstances, to say the least, so it is a beautiful thing to pull into the driveway of his home. He definitely worked his ass off to get where he is today, and, I know, if no one else knows, that his road to victory was a rough one. While my mom and dad busted their asses to take care of me and Olivia, Scott's mother, a single parent, cared more about her boyfriends, than Scott's welfare. I swear, that woman, doesn't deserve to be called a mother.

Scott's mother's boyfriends probably had more fun with Scott, than they did with his mother. And I recall when Scott tried to tell his mother about one man in particular, I believe his name was Everett, and she didn't want to hear shit. She ended up blaming Scott for trying to take her boyfriend away from her, rather than being a mother to her child, and not only did she not acknowledge the molestation, she said Scott wanted it. Scott and I became so very close during his hard times, and for that, I am grateful; not that he went through the turmoil, just that I was able to help him get through it all. We have an unbelievably, unbreakable bond.

A slight tap on the horn signals Scott that we're here. I know better than to blow the horn too loud for him. Meanwhile, Keisha's ghetto-ass, rolls down the window, sticks her head out, and yells, "Hey punk ass, bring your bitch ass downstairs, we here."

"Keisha!"

"What, Amber?"

"Now you know…"

"Know what, Amber? Scott ain't gon' do shit but bring his high yellow, faggot ass downstairs and get his ass in the backseat. And yes, I said, in the backseat. That's where he likes it any damn way, back door ass ho."

A look of disbelief crosses my face as I prepare to respond to Keisha's last statement, but Scott's abrupt walk to the car distracts me. Here he comes, man-bag in hand, Versace shades perfectly planted on his face, crisp and clean blue jeans and a pristine white button up. He looks pissed too.

My attempt to get out of the car to greet Scott with a kiss is unsuccessful, as he rushes over, and firmly plants me back on my ass in the driver's seat.

"Uh uh, baby girl, sit down. I don't want you doing too much." He kisses me on the cheek, and continues. "Are you feeling okay?"

"Yes, I'm fine, Scott."

"Do you want me to drive, Amber?"

"No, Scott, I'm good. Get in, so we can get to the doctor. You know I don't want to be late."

"Okay."

As Scott walks across the front of the car, his eyes are glued to his arch nemesis, Keisha. He moves in, close to the passenger seat, where Keisha is sitting, taps on the window. Keisha rolls it down, and the clairvoyant in her is expelled, as she tells Scott, before he gets a chance to say anything, "No, bitch, get your ass in the back seat, 'cause I ain't movin'."

Scott lowers his shades, looking pass Keisha and straight at me. "I'm only doing this for you, Amber. Not for this black stallion." He looks at Keisha and continues. "Give that horse his hair back. You know you're really not a stallion, right, Keisha? You really need to let some of that weave-a-licious hair go."

Keisha rolls the window up in the middle of Scott's last statement. I cover my mouth so as not to laugh out loud.

My peripheral vision allows me to see Scott's finger, as it approaches, landing in between me and Keisha. Keisha turns around to yell at him. "What, bitch? Damn, do you ever shut the fuck up, Scott?"

"Now, see bitch. I'll deal with your jet-black ass later. I was going to tell you two bitches to take that R. Kelly CD OUT of the player, because I don't listen to niggas that piss on girls who ain't got their diplomas yet."

It's going to be a long day.

We arrive at Dr. Henderson's office, deep in the heart of Newark— a new medical office complex. Lord knows, I don't know why I still come here. If I have an appointment at two in the afternoon, I won't see Dr. Henderson until six in the evening. I pray today is different, because honestly, I just don't have time to sit and wait, and wait and sit, especially when both Scott and Keisha are present.

A silent prayer escapes me as I turn the doorknob, hoping the waiting room does not resemble the ghetto factory assembly line it normally looks like. We all walk in, and my worst nightmare is now reality, as the waiting room is filled to capacity with wall-to-wall coochies. Scott and Keisha both look me up and down. Scott pushes us to the side, and opens the door to enter the patient exam rooms. The nurse practitioner rushes over. A small, chubby Haitian woman confronts Scott, and blocks his path.

"May I help you?"

"No, Aunt Jemima, you can't, but Amber Devereaux is here and needs to be seen right away."

Taking obvious offense to Scott's comment, she responds, "Sir, have a seat, and we'll call you when we're ready."

Scott turns around to look at Keisha and me, with a no-she-didn't look, and signals for me to come over. Keisha can't help herself.

"No he is not waving that damn, fragile, long ass finger!"

"Shut up, Kunta, and get your ass over here!"

We both arrive to Scott, and he pushes the nurse out of the way and yells for Dr. Henderson.

"Yoo hoo, Dr. Henderson, Amber is here. She's pregnant and needs to be seen right away."

The nurse approaches Scott, not looking too happy. "We'll take her, but you and this woman here cannot come in the exam room."

Scott leans in, to get all of the nurse's undivided attention. "We're all going into that exam room today, sweets." He points to me. "This here is Amber." He points to himself. "I'm the baby daddy." He points to Keisha. "And this here...oh, she's the seeing-eye dog."

The nurse smiles and Keisha hits Scott on the arm. The nurse leads us into Exam Room Two. I've never been able to get in here this quick in my life. I guess Scott has a way of persuading people, either that, or she had no time to deal with his flamboyant ass.

As I enter the exam room, I see the nurse place the paper towel robe on the examining table. I turn around to make sure Keisha and Scott are out of the room, so that I'll be able to take off my clothes in privacy. No sooner than I turn around, Scott tells me, "No, bitch. I'm not leaving. You can tell Keisha to go if you want to, but I need to make sure good ole Dr. Henderson takes good care of my Godchild." The look I give him is one of disbelief, because I love his gay ass to death, but he's not staying in this exam room with me. Scott has lost his mind.

"Nigga, you done bumped yo' punk ass head, twinkle toes. How you look stayin' in here while the doctor all up in Amber's coochie?" Keisha says while making her black ass comfortable in the chair next to the table.

"Keisha, you're not staying in here either," I tell her, hoping that the two of them would leave immediately.

Scott takes chair number two, and slides it in front of him, unbuttons a few buttons on the top part of his shirt, and takes a seat. "You're right, Keisha. I did bump my head…on your man's dick last night. And yes, midnight, I will be staying."

Keisha snarls, while Scott sticks his tongue out. This shit can't be real. I yell to both of them to get out.

Five minutes later, my cold ass is laying flat on my back, feet in stirrups, exposed via frontal nudity, and all that covers me is a piece of shit, flimsy, paper towel robe. After my breast exam, Dr. Henderson heads down south to give me an internal exam, to check on the baby. And yes, Scott and Keisha are both on either side of Dr. Henderson. I guess as of way of showing their support. The truth is stranger than fiction.

"So, how are you feeling, Amber?"

"I'm feeling just fine, Dr. Henderson."

He takes his gloves off. That five-second internal was more than enough, and I'm sure my beet-red face expresses the same.

"Uh, baby girl, you need to shave," Scott says to me, as Dr. Henderson is finishing up.

"You have very interesting friends, Amber," Dr. Henderson smirks.

"I know."

"That's 'cause we love your high yellow ass, Amber. Damn, girl, you really are pure as the driven snow. I didn't know how light you really are until your ass in the flesh, girl," Keisha says and laughs out loud.

"Okay, we'll see you back here in about a month. We'll do your ultrasound then."

As Dr. Henderson prepares to walk out of the exam room, I lean up and prepare to get dressed. Scott must be reading my mind, because he questions the doctor be he could get through the door good. "Excuse me, Dr. Henderson?"

"Yes?"

"Hypothetically speaking. If a woman is, let's say, umm, six to eight weeks pregnant, and has fucked two men within a two- to four-week period, is there any way to determine who the father is?"

Keisha's eyes almost pop out of their sockets. My eyes roll to the back of my head and a cold sweat flushes me. Scott looks at both Keisha and me, with a yes-I-did-say-it look, and yes, we're all ears.

"Well, it's hard to tell, because this is not an exact science. The only way to know for sure is to have a test done to determine who the father is. Believe it or not, the mother, in many cases knows who the father of their child is."

Khalil
Machine Gun Funk

It's been a few weeks since I got to hang out with my boy, Shawn. He kind of disappeared after the whole Aaliyah fiasco. I fell back, let him do his thang, in his own time, and gave him his space. Told him I was here if he needed me—to talk, to hang out, chill, whatever. I know he was in love with Aaliyah and fell for her real hard. Going through that kind of turmoil, agony and pain over a love lost had to be difficult for my man. But, Shawn is strong, so I know he'll be all right. Laughing out loud was the only thing I could do after all that bullshit went down. If I didn't find the shit amusing, I would've broken Shayla's ass in two. So glad I'll be getting my daughter soon, even if its just for a week or so, just so she'll be able to get a break from the monotony; get out of her ghetto ass mother's clutches. Bringing her around Amber will do Lex some good.

As I pull up to my man's loft, I smile again, reminiscing about that day on the front steps, when Shawn kicked Aaliyah's ass out of town. Ha! The shit still makes me laugh. I was scared shitless on that day too, because that was the day Amber found out about my dirt. Thank goodness, Shawn was there to comfort her. After a few beeps of the horn, Shawn comes out, gym bag in hand, a big ass white tee, some sweats and sneakers. Same shit

I have on. Once again, we are headed to the NY Sports Club, to get our work out on, just like the good ole days. I pop the locks for my boy and he hops into my new ride.

"I likes, I likes, baby!" Shawn smiles, gives me a pound, and makes himself comfortable in the passenger side of my new H2.

"It's hot, right?" I ask him, as he brushes the leather and wood grain with his hand, still cheesin'.

"Definitely, a hot ride, man."

"So, let's head over to the gym, get our workout on, and then grab some lunch. You down with that?"

"No doubt."

Riding through the streets of Manhattan, mid-day is somewhat of a challenge, but I got this shit covered. Just a few more blocks, and we'll be there. A cool, fall-winter like day in the City brings out some of New York's finest. Thank God I'm a changed man. I have to fuck with Shawn at this point.

"Damn." I point to the honey walking across the street. She's a redbone mami, sporting a baby phat jacket and some blue jeans and high-heeled boots.

"What, man?" Shawn responds questioningly.

"Check out honey-dip crossing the street."

Shawn doesn't respond, instead faces his window to glance out of it, and rolls the window down. He's pretending like he's sincerely interested in what's going on out there. I think I touched a nerve, given his Aaliyah dilemma. I offer consolation.

"Look man, I'm sorry. I thought you were over Aaliyah, man."

He looks at me like I've just fucked his mother, and father. "Man, I ain't thought about Aaliyah since I kicked her ass out of my home, and life. But are you serious, man?"

"About?"

"Are you still looking at other women, K? After the shit you just went through? You almost lost your wife, for good, I might add. You almost lost, Amber."

Shawn's tone is way too serious, and doesn't evenly match my silly comment about the chick crossing the street. Something's up, and I plan to find out what.

"Yo, Shawn. I was just fucking around, man."

"Whatever, man."

"What the fuck is wrong with you, Shawn?"

"Nothing man. Just some people don't know how blessed they are, that's all I'm saying. But you got your wife back, so it's all good."

"Yeah, I got her back. But things ain't all good. And why you so emotional about it, Shawn?"

"I ain't emotional, K. I'm just telling you that any man would be happy to be in your shoes. I don't think I've ever told you that. We never discussed that part of your relationship. The part about how fucking blessed you are to have a woman like Amber."

"I know how blessed I am, which is why I ain't fucking around. And let me remind you that I haven't cheated on Amber since we've been married."

"Not yet, anyway."

"What? Shawn, I don't want to argue with your ass today."

"So, don't. And what do you mean 'shit ain't all good' between you and Amber?"

"Nothing man."

"Come on, K. What's up?"

"She just ain't been right since that day. Since she found out about those strippers. She cries all the time; she won't let me touch her. It's real weird. But I'm going to stay strong and stay by her side. I ain't letting Amber go. I know she loves me, and I plan on proving to her everyday, just how sorry I am for hurting her."

"I see."

I see is not the answer I expected from Shawn. He normally has a fucking lecture prepared for me for talks like this. Not today. He's just bobbin' his head to an old Notorious B.I.G. classic, *Machine Gun Funk* and enjoying the ride. And in true Shawn Fontaine fashion, he comes back, revealing his true self again.

"But honey was fine as hell, K. Did you see that booty?"

We both break out into laughter, but Shawn ain't catching me out there, not again.

"Yeah, she was, but Shawn, I ain't sayin' shit else. All I see is Amber!"

We laugh again.

Shawn sings along to Biggie, "The funk, baby."

"So, how are you handling the Aaliyah thing?"

"I'm good, Khalil, really. It wasn't meant for me, that's all. Hopefully, I'll get what's coming to me."

"I'm sure you will, brother."

Shawn admires my H2's interior. "Yo, man, how much this set you back?"

"About, fifty G's."

"Good deal. Yo, K, did I tell you about Summer?"

"Who?"

"Summer Rain. Yes, that's her name. Scott introduced the two of us. Gave her my phone number. She needed some financial help. Man, voice smooth and sexy. She just sound like she can fuck."

"Damn, word? So, Scott's punk ass is good for something, huh?"

"Apparently so."

"Anyway, I had a business meeting with her once, and we've been talking on the phone for a while now. Man, she knows everything about me. She asked me out. So we're going out to dinner tonight."

"She fine?"

"Yeah. Nice and thick. Light-skinned, long hair. Nice ass. Big tits. She smart too, yo."

"Word? My man got his groove back, huh?"

"We'll see what happens. I'll take it real slow. I don't want to rush anything. She the shit, but I thought Aaliyah was the shit."

Shawn takes a deep breath, leans back in the passenger seat, reclining the seat back more, putting his hand behind his head and confesses in a somber tone, "I ain't been right since that day."

Finally, we make it to the sports club, and thankfully, it's pretty empty inside, which is why we always choose a weekday to come, early in the day too. I'm feeling this shit too. I had to reduce my pace on the treadmill; it's been a minute. Shawn's head is dripping sweat and he keeps his speed. I'm down to a light jog, and will build up speed momentarily. As Shawn grabs his white towel from the railing on the treadmill, I spark a small conversation. It's good news, and I'm sure he'll be happy to hear it.

"Guess what?"

"What, man?" Shawn looks at me through sweat covered eyes.

"Lex is coming up for a week?"

"Really? That's what's up, man. Do the right thing by your child."

"Yeah, I had to step up to the plate. Become a real man, and its working. Thanks to you and Amber. I'm sure Amber would like to thank you for helping me on my journey to manhood."

A slight smirk escapes Shawn's lips. As he continues to keep his pace on the treadmill, he manages to get these words out, "I'm sure Lex will be happy to have some time with her daddy. It's important, K."

"Yeah, I know, Shawn. I had to threaten Shayla about joint custody, before she said okay."

"Yeah, that Shayla is a piece of work, K. Glad you finally left that tramp alone."

"Me too, brother, me too."

We're both down to a walk on the treadmills now. And head over to the weight benches. I ask Shawn to spot me.

"I don't know how I will get back into Amber's good graces, Shawn."

"It'll work out the way it's supposed to, Khalil. Give her some time. Do something sweet for her. She likes to be held and caressed. Try that, and maybe light some candles."

"What?" Shawn's knowledge of my woman's wants and desires, likes and dislikes throws me for a loop. I am now finding it hard to get this weight off my chest.

"I meant, just do something romantic for her. You know how sensitive Amber is."

Khalil
Keep the Lights On

It's pretty chilly out here, for real, which makes me so happy to be done with all my meetings today—no more bouncing from here to there on this frosty, winter-kissed evening. Its time to get home. As I climb into the driver's side of my Escalade, I feel good as the heat is bumpin' nice and Gerald Levert's *G Spot* CD matches equally to the mood I'm in, which is grown and sexy, loving and in need of love. As the soulful voice encircles the truck, I can only pray that God rests his soul. I also think of the love of my life, the reason for my existence, my soul mate, Amber.

Remembering all of the times I've done my woman wrong, nothing but regret resurfaces and my nerves become uneasy and anxious. This time may have been the one that forces me to lose everything, but I refuse. I refuse to give up. Refuse to let my marriage end, go astray. I am so sorry Amber found out about the bachelor party and I promise, on my grandmother's grave, I will never hurt my wife again. I simply love her too much. I just pray she finds it in her heart to forgive me and my dumb ass indiscretion. Knowing Amber, she will eventually one day allow this to be a horrible bad memory, but right now she is making sure I fully understand the consequences of my actions. I swear, growing up, becoming a real man, and accepting responsibility for myself has me sounding so much like Shawn. That's not a bad thing. It's just strange.

Reaching over to press speed dial on my phone, which is propped up on the dashboard, I think of her. My lady, my baby, Amber. I hope she picks up. It's so weird, she doesn't raise her voice to me or even behave like a woman scorned, with the tantrums and fighting. She's very calm, which is scary, but that's Amber. She's making me pay, in her own special way. I can't remember the last time I made love to her.

Every night, crawling into bed with my beautiful wife, all I can think of is making love to her, especially when she's freshly showered. She smells so damn good; I want to devour her pussy, with a passion, as soon as she walks out the bathroom. But I can't. She has a subtle way of giving me the "you ain't gettin' none of this ass" look. Yeah, I want to make love to her so badly, but tonight, right now, at this moment, I could fuck the shit out of Amber. I'm lonely, horny and don't want nothing but my wife.

I press 123, which is Amber's speed dial code on my phone. I eagerly await the sweet and sexy voice to greet me on the other end. The butterflies in my stomach are fluttering like crazy. It's eight-thirty in the evening so I know she's home. She mentioned getting a manicure and pedicure today and said she'd be home around five or six. Okay, she picks up.

"Hello?"

"Hey, baby."

"Hi, Khalil."

Silence.

I clear my throat.

"How are you feeling, baby?"

"I'm fine, Khalil, thanks for asking."

I hate this. I need to reconnect with her. "Do you need anything, Amber? I'm on my way home now."

"No, Khalil, I'm just fine. I went grocery shopping earlier."

"Okay. Would you like some dessert?"

"I have some, Khalil. And dinner is done."

"Did you eat already Amber?"

"No, I haven't, Khalil."

"You didn't have to wait for me."

"Uh huh."

No matter what we're going through, Amber always makes a great meal for me, keeps the house pristine, and treats me like a King. I know Mother Clark taught her that. Most hood rat bitches out here would be fucking my best friend by now.

"Uh huh, what Amber?"

"Nothing, Khalil."

"I love you, Amber."

"Okay, Khalil."

"Amber!"

"Yes, Khalil."

"Talk to me, please."

"There's nothing else to say. Dinner is ready. I'll see you when you get home."

"Am–"

Click.

Damn, she actually hung up on me. I guess I deserve it. But she's pissing me the hell off now. I fucked up. I know this. I'm working hard as hell to make this right, but she ain't making it easy for a brother.

Parking in front of the building, I pop Gerald's *G Spot* out and return it to its case. I grab my briefcase, detach my cell phone, step out of the truck and throw on my full length Sean Jean. A brother's got to stay warm. I lock up the truck and head to our condo.

Inserting the key in the door, I slowly turn the knob and the aroma from the kitchen bitch slaps me right in the face. I'm hungry as hell too. Its going down tonight. Smells like Amber made my favorite meal.

I walk further into our condo and see its spotless, as usual, and Amber is sitting on the living room sofa watching *24*, one of her favorite shows. Damn, it's after nine o'clock already. Walking up slowly to the sofa, I reach down and give Amber a smooch on her cheek and she abruptly gets off the sofa and walks into the kitchen. And while doing so, I notice the beautiful perfection that is my wife. Damn.

My eyes follow her from behind as she walks by wearing a floor length burgundy silk robe. I can't dare blink for fear I may lose sight of her delicious ass. Look at them cakes shake as she walks slowly, tempting me with what I won't be getting. Damn, she's fucking with me and she knows it. Her fresh, French-pedicure looks great on her feet in her fury slippers and the aroma of her White Diamonds perfume flows lightly in mid-air, penetrating my nostrils.

I loosen my tie and throw it on the floor, place my briefcase and coat near the coffee table. I sit at the head of our dining room table where Amber has candles lit. Still keeping my eyes on her every move, she walks slowly toward me from the kitchen with a glass of sangria, which she knows is my favorite drink, with my favorite meal; baked ziti filled with ground turkey, Italian sausage, roasted garlic, fresh tomatoes and three cheeses. She even made fresh asparagus and garlic bread, fresh out of the oven.

As she walks toward me, I can't help but notice the silky flow of her hair as it glides past her shoulders, parted in the middle and beveled to both sides. She must've gone to the beauty parlor today. And look at her skin, so silky smooth, rich and soft, and I want to fuck her right now. And she doesn't have a bra on either because those nipples are rising like they're in a civil rights movement, as her pretty tits bounce in beat to that sexy swagger. She reaches me. I sip my sangria.

"Thank you, Amber."

"You're welcome, Khalil."

She sits next to me and begins to eat.

"This food is so good, baby. And I love the sangria."

"Thank you, Khalil."

"You're not having any sangria, baby?"

"Not today, Khalil. I'm cool."

"Did you get your hair done?"

"Yes, I did."

"It looks really good, baby."

"Thanks, Khalil."

As I devour this excellent meal and work on my third glass of sangria, I visualize kissing Amber slowly, tasting those sweet lips once again. I imagine becoming reacquainted with my woman all over again. I want her so fucking bad. She has to know this. I make mindless conversation just to get her to talk to me.

"How was work today, baby?"

"I didn't go to work today, Khalil. I took the day off."

"Did you? Is everything okay?"

"Yes."

"So, why did you take the day off? You normally tell me these things."

"Well, seems like we don't behave *normally* these days, Khalil."

"Listen, Amb–"

She cuts me off.

"I had a doctor's appointment, then I went to get a manicure and pedicure, a facial and my hair washed."

"You look beautiful, baby."

Silence, but she appears to have blushed slightly.

There is a God.

We finish our meal and I just want to chill and cuddle up with my woman. Amber clears the table and attempts to walk away when I grab her by the arm and softly kiss her hand, stealing remnants of her scent, before she snatches away.

"I miss you, Amber."

She takes the plates into the kitchen, runs the water and fills the sink with Dove as she prepares to clean. Fuck this. I can't help myself. I carefully tiptoe into the kitchen and walk up behind her. Pressing up against her, she feels so fucking good right now. I haven't been this close to her in ages.

I push in closer so that it becomes hard for her to move away from me. She has no choice but to let me feel her. I lean in, smell the freshness of her hair, feel her butter-soft face. I kiss her cheek. I feel her exhale. She's trying to resist but she's not going to win tonight. I need her too badly.

I softly whisper in her ear, "Amber, I love you so much. Baby, please, I need you."

She doesn't respond but I can see her nipples rising through her robe, wanting my attention. They look divine. My dick swells and becomes thick instantly.

She attempts to wash the dishes when I reach into the sink and take her hands into mine, rub up her arms with the warm, soapy dishwater. She exhales again. Her nipples are hard as tiny pebbles. I love the sight of those Tootsie Roll nipples and can't wait to get my lips around them.

I hope I don't hurt her because she's going to get it tonight. I'm gonna lay it on her sweet ass if I have my way.

"Amber, please. Don't push me away. Let me talk to you for a minute."

She doesn't respond but puts up less of a fight.

I turn her around and take her by the hand, lead her to the sofa and sit her down. I turn off the television so that I can have her undivided attention. All that illuminates the floor are the candles from the dining room table.

She won't look me in the eyes, so I gently grab her chin and turn her face toward me.

"Amber, baby, I am *so sorry* for hurting you. I love you *so* much. I need your forgiveness, baby."

Again, she doesn't respond.

"Amber, I miss you so much. Please forgive me. I love you, baby."

I inch in toward her scrumptious mouth and lick her lips, bite them, and place my tongue into her mouth and she tries to resist but opens up for me. I kiss her passionately, allowing my tongue to become reacquainted with her loveliness and my fingertips softly brush her chest, her abdomen, I rub her thighs. I'm ready to explode.

I've always been a forceful, lustful lover with Amber because there's so much to enjoy. I can't help myself. I'm going to try to be sweet and gentle but it's going to be hard as hell because I want her so damn bad.

Fuck it.

Removing my tongue from her mouth, I kiss her cheek and whisper in her ear once more. "Do you miss me, baby?"

Her breathing is heavy and that glazed euphoria in her eyes tells me she wants me just as much as I want her.

She doesn't respond.

I kiss her neck and reach her other ear as my hands caress her nipples.

"Because I miss you so much, Amber."

She exhales.

Kissing her neck, her chin, down her chest, my tongue finds its way to her breast and I release it from its silk prison. Her nipples are at attention, as I go to work on them with gentle bites and deep tongue kisses.

"Amber, hold your breasts together for me."

She obliges.

"Good girl."

She begins to moan as I playfully tease her nipples with my tongue, alternating between both breasts until she can't take it anymore.

I slide to my knees and kneel in front of her. Unloosening the belt to her robe exposes soft, butterscotch skin that smells divine. I need to eat her pussy.

"Amber, spread your pussy real nasty for me, baby."

She obliges.

"Damn, Amber, your pussy looks so fucking good. Its so pretty. Can I eat it baby?"

"Yes, Khalil. Please eat it."

Taking the palms of my hands, I spread her legs as far as they'll go and stick my tongue in her pussy and fuck her with it.

"Oooh, Khalil. I can't…God, its so good."

I take my fingers and suck them, fuck her with them and suck on her clit.

"Khalil, you're going to make me cum."

"Cum, Amber, please. Cum on my mouth."

I aggressively lick the walls of her soft, cushiony sex and eat her pussy like I'll never get to do this again. My fingers play with her clit as I fuck her more with my tongue and smack her ass a few times to get them juices flowing real nice.

"Shit, Khalil, I'm cummin'."

This sweet pussy starts to cream right before my eyes and I know I've made my impact. Looking up at her gorgeous face, her mouth open and her eyes tells me she's ready for me and that's what I want to do; give her more. *I want to fuck the sense out of her.*

"Come on, baby. Let's go upstairs, Amber."

Taking her by her hand, I follow her to the staircase and admire her full ass as I see her cheeks bounce underneath the silk sheath. She reaches around and looks back at me, but doesn't say a word. The seductress in her has come out to play and makes me impatient as I can't wait to get upstairs to our bedroom to feel her pussy wrap tightly around my dick. *Hold it hostage, goddamnit.*

The anticipation makes me stop dead in my tracks. I tug at her arm.

"Amber, wait."

Bending her over one of the steps, I spread her legs, unbutton my pants and allow them to drop to my ankles. I rub her ass as I admire how good it looks and smack it. One cheek at a time.

"Damn, Amber."

I remove her robe and toss it over the staircase. While admiring her full body of perfection, I'm happy as hell I drank so much tonight, because if I hadn't, I'd cum in about thirty seconds.

She looks back at me again, while she's bent over and I can see those tits bouncing as she shakes her ass in anticipation of me. I finger her pussy some more to get it ready for me.

She's so fucking drenched. Mmmm.

I spread her ass real nice and wide and place my tip into her sweetness.

"Shit, Amber, you so wet, baby."

"Ooh, Khalil, please give it to me."

I'll give it to you, alright.

Giving her tip, then shaft, then pulling out to tip only makes her gyrate and quiver, and let out moans that make my dick harder inside of her. I give it all to her, inserting deeper than I've ever been before, down deep into the depths of her sweetness and her sugary walls grab a hold of me.

She's so tight; I feel like I'm poppin' her cherry for the first time.

"Ooh, Amber, give it to me."

"Ah, ah, ah, Khalil, its so good baby. Fuck me nice and slow, Khalil, please."

"Yeah baby, throw that ass back to me, Amber. Come on, baby."

"Mmmm."

"Amber, this still my pussy, right?"

"All yours, Khalil."

"Mmm. That's a good girl."

The deeper I go, the more I feel like I better slow this down. This tight, wet, hot pussy is going to make me cum all over the place if I don't get a grip.

"Let's go upstairs, Amber."

"Khalil! Please don't take it from me."

"I promise baby, you will get it all when we get in bed."

I slowly pull out and notice how shiny, wet and saturated my dick is as it points straight ahead, as if I'm going up to yonder, as we head to the bedroom.

Amber lights the candles and turns the lights off.

"Uh uh, Amber. Blow those candles out. Keep the lights on baby."

I finish removing my clothes and allow them to drop to the floor and lay on my back, onto our king-sized massive bed. I reach out for Amber to join me and she does, nipples still rock solid and those fine pussy hairs still glossy. She takes my hand and I pull her close to me.

"Ride me, Amber."

She straddles me as I grab her hips to position her.

"Put it in that sweet pussy, Amber."

Those perfectly manicured fingers look good as hell as they grab hold of me as I enter into that pretty pink hole once more. She slides down onto me and the pleasure we've been seeking all night greets us once more. She can barely say a word and neither can I.

"Ooh, Khalil."

"Amber, ride me good, baby. Fuck me like you love me. It's your dick, baby."

She obliges and rides Daddy nice and slow allowing me a sensual visual of my pipe in and out of her delight, over and over again. I grab hold of her tits and play with her nipples then hold on to her hips as I delve deeper and deeper into this first-class pussy.

"Amber, I love you."

I stroke her hard.

Her head tilts back.

"Amber, I love you so much."

I'm fucking her harder, deeper.

Her back arches, head falls back again.

"Amber, I love you, baby."

She releases all over me, brings her face back into view where the tears roll down her cheeks.

I'm going buck wild now, fucking her as hard as I can and the flood from her tears lands on my chest. With one of my deepest blows, she moves the Earth from beneath me.

"Khalil! Not so deep. Don't hurt the baby!"

Everything stops.

Dead silence.

The tears now pour relentlessly from my eyes as I respond to my beautiful wife. "What did you say?"

"Don't hurt the baby, Khalil."

"Amber, are you pregnant, baby?" I ask as I pull her off of me, lay next to her, kiss her lips, kiss her belly, put my ear to her stomach, come back to her face; kiss her some more. I can taste our mixed teardrops in my mouth as I prepare to speak but my emotions consume me whole. I lay on her breasts.

"I'm pregnant, Khalil."

Summer

Satisfaction Brought Him Back

I follow his sexy swagger as he walks slightly ahead of me, to open the door. He looks sincerely divine in black slacks that tug at his firm track star booty, ever so gently. His butter-soft leather, three-quarter-inch jacket, offsets his enticing black skin, giving him a sexy and warm, piping hot look this evening. How he looks when he's business only, in no way compares to the beauty of his stature when he's out on an official date. Brother put it down tonight, from the pickup at my apartment, to the flowers he had in tow; lovely yellow roses, with one white one, he said was for me, because I'm one of a kind; this man is serious, so much so, that all of my previous fantasies and daydreams about Mr. Fontaine, will hopefully, I pray, come to life tonight. I'm wanting him in the worst way.

We arrive at Fresh Waters, a soul food restaurant, about twenty minutes from my home. So nice of Shawn to come to Jersey this evening. I told him that I didn't mind catching the train into the city, but he insisted. Said it was gentlemanly of him to drive me around, and take me wherever I wanted to go, on him, he added. I hope he's ready to go to Utopia, because I got a first-class ticket set aside for his ass.

"Thank you, Shawn." I look over my right shoulder, my eyes scanning his broad shoulders, moving up to his sinfully luscious lips, which are surrounded by a divine, perfectly trimmed goatee. An ultra masculine physique, Shawn stands tall and statuesque, and his deep, dark brown mysterious eyes pull me in, luring me delicately. I scroll down to the delectable smile of pure white teeth as he opens the door of the restaurant for me.

"You're quite welcome, Summer." He follows behind me, closely. So close in fact, that I feel the warmth of his breath land on my cheek.

The hostess greets us. "Hi, welcome to Fresh Waters, do you have reservations?" She grabs two menus from the podium. Her eyes light up as she checks Shawn out, on the low, and I can't blame her, because his ass is fine. But, that shit is making me mad as hell right now. Oh shit, her eyes constantly follow his every move and jealousy has set in on my part.

As polite and dignified as he is, Shawn responds, "Yes, two under Shawn Fontaine," as he takes my hand in his.

"Great, follow me."

We reach our booth, which is seductively situated in a nice corner of the restaurant. He takes my coat as I plant my ass firmly into the booth, but not before bending over slightly to give him a visual of what's soon to come, if he's down for a nice ride. To make my attraction undeniable, I accidentally, on purpose, drop my handbag to the floor, and bend all of the way over to pick it up, slowly. Slowly pulling myself up, I take my coat from him and place it on the side. "Thank you, dear," I smile as he takes his seat.

"So, I've moved up a notch, you called me dear." The sexiest grin I've ever seen turn up at the corner of Shawn's juicy lips.

"You're at the top of my list, Mr. Fontaine." I smile, giving him an equally inviting parting of my lips. "You landed at number one the first day I spoke with you."

"Is that right?"

Reaching my hand over to his, I gently caress it and rub it. "Yes, it is."

"I'll keep that in mind, Summer. I feel honored to be at the top," Shawn tells me, while reciprocating the rub I just offered to his silky smooth hand. His very touch sends shock waves through me. I love the way he looks, the way he feels.

"How's number one sound to you?"

As he lifts the corners of his mouth with a smile that melts me all the way through, he answers me with, "Number one sounds good to me."

"Good. Because that's where you are, Shawn."

Taking my hand, he kisses the back of it, and his lips are so very soft and smooth, as his hot breath penetrates my skin. "I like that, Summer." He kisses it again. My walls are on fire, and I feel a pounding ache between my legs. I'm squirming in my seat, and I hope he can't see my reactions to his every move.

Our eyes begin to make love to one another, pulling the two of us into a deep trance, so much so, that the waitress tells us that she'll come back later to take our orders. I see passion in his eyes.

With the boldness of a cobra, I ask, "What do you have planned for tonight?" as I stroke the inside of the palm of his hand with my index finger, indicating just what I want him to plan, with me. A night of some serious, getting to know you fucking. As my finger makes tiny circles to his inner palm, he smiles, parting his lips slowly, and I see him exhale. His body shudders, the more I do it.

"How about I let you make the plans?" he tells me, smiling from ear to ear. Reciprocating my index finger move, he tickles my inner palm with his long finger. Orgasmic pulses shoot through my arm, towards my shoulders. The pulsing sensation travels down my chest and belly, settling between my thighs.

Just as I am about to send shockwaves back at him, his cell rings.

"Oh sorry, Summer, I thought I turned my phone off." He extends his hand to his waist to retrieve his phone. "I'll grab this call and then, I promise, I'll turn the phone off."

"Okay, Shawn, no problem."

The look on his face is one of disgust. Oh my, I hope all is well.

"Aaliyah, don't call me anymore," he whispers and looks at me like a sad puppy dog. Gently closing the flip to his phone, he turns it off, places it into the pocket of his jacket and offers an apology. "I'm sorry. That was my ex. I told you about her. She won't be an intrusion for much longer."

"No problem, Shawn. I can relate to her begging though," I tell him, knowing good and damn well that no, it's not okay that she is calling. Trying to suppress my jealousy is not easy.

"Yeah?"

"Absolutely. You're a good man. I'm sure she's regretting her past decisions."

"Probably so. Well, let's not waste anytime on her. I'm all yours tonight."

"That sounds dangerous, Shawn, and I'm all yours as long as you're all mine."

I want to fuck the life out of him.

The waitress returns with a smile to her face. "Are you two lovebirds ready to order?"

Shawn looks at me. "Are you ready Summer?"

"I'll have whatever you're having, Shawn."

"Okay then. Yes, we'll have two of your catfish and shrimp dinners, with macaroni and cheese, collard greens, cornbread and two lemonades," he tells the waitress and hands her the two menus.

"Good choices," I smile at, while rubbing my foot across his calf.

Shawn smiles at my sensuous jester of what to know him better. "You look beautiful this evening, Summer."

"Thank you, Shawn. You look good as hell tonight yourself." My toe is rubbing his calf and he smiles each time I move up his leg a little more. Shawn sips his water, and I continue rubbing as I play with my napkin.

"Ha, ha. You're cute. I like a woman who is unafraid to speak her mind."

"Well then, you've got the right one, Shawn."

"Is that right?"

"If you want it to be, Shawn, yes, you have the right one. Are you ready for that?"

"Maybe."

Trying not to force the issue or seem too desperate, I switch gears. He's just come out of a heart-wrenching situation and I don't want to push it. I think Shawn may want to change the subject too, as he has gone on to another subject entirely.

"So, Summer, you were telling me the flipside to working for Immigration. I don't see why people can't come to this country to form a better life."

"You have a valid concern, Shawn. My job is in deportation. And I get that question a lot. What we do is deport the not so good immigrants."

"But, they're people of color, right, Summer? That's the part I don't like."

"But Shawn, what you don't know is that they are not the 'I want the American Dream' immigrants. These men have rap sheets as long as your arm. Everything from child molestation, to rape and murder. In their countries, that underage sex thing is big, and they try to do that shit over here. You would think murder, drugs and rape of women are the biggest issues when deporting them. It's not. It is molestation and underage sex with young girls, as young as five."

Shawn's eyes open as wide as my heart is for him now. That jaw dropping information is what most people don't know or realize.

"Wow, I had no clue," he tells me and takes a sip of his lemonade.

"It's all good, Shawn. That's the one thing I love about my job. At least I can make a difference in some sort of capacity."

"I hear you."

The sweet sounds of *The Quiet Storm* offers a delightful background to an already seductive setting, and a cozy ride back to my place. The music plays so softly, as Shawn hums the tunes of Jamie Foxx's *Unpredictable*. I boldly take this opportunity to introduce Shawn to my inner thighs. Taking his hand, I place it onto my left thigh, and steer it up and down, round and round to feel how soft and silky it is beneath my skirt. That sexy curl of his lips signal to me that he likes this. I return the favor, and rub my hand up his thigh, and lean in to his right ear, licking the lobe.

"Mmm, Summer, you've got my attention."

"Good, Shawn. I've been dying to get your undivided attention all night."

After a lovely evening of dinner, we now rest our behinds on the sofa in my living room. I make the two of us nightcaps of Bailey's and we enjoy them, while listening to Sade.

"Her words are so befitting for this moment." As Sade sings, *Is it a crime?* I begin to sing out loud. "That I still want you, and I want you to want me too."

"You have a nice place here, Summer, and a beautiful voice," he tells me as he runs his feet through my plush carpet.

"Thank you, Shawn."

I get up from the sofa to pour another drink of Bailey's. "Would you like another?" I ask, while taking his empty glass away.

"Sure," he replies, getting up from the sofa. "On second thought, Summer, I don't want to drink too much. I do have a ride back into the city tonight."

"I see."

His eyebrows raise, sensing my obvious and blatant disappointment, and Shawn comes over to me in the kitchen. Walking up to me, he touches my shoulder. "Look Summer."

Placing a single finger over his lips, I tell him, "I know. I'm moving too fast. I'll back off."

Grabbing my other shoulder, he looks deep into my eyes. "It's not that. You're a beautiful woman. It's just that my heart is a bit complicated right now."

"I understand, Shawn. But do you have to go now?"

"No, I don't, I just don't want to get drunk. My heart may be in turmoil and confused at the moment, but I'm not blind, Summer."

Looking up to him, I ask, "What do you mean, Shawn?"

"I mean, Summer, that you are a very attractive woman." He bends down to give me a luscious kiss. "And I love your lips."

"Thank you," I blush.

"And I love your smile," he tells me as he helps me to pour another glass of Bailey's for myself. "And I love your neck. Especially this spot right here." He kisses my neck softly. The touch of his lips on my neck is so erotic.

"Thank you, Shawn."

Putting down the glass of Baileys, I move in close to him, giving him a hug. Wow, he really feels good, as his back is so strong and muscular, and damn, his chest is so broad and sexy. He smells just like I imagined. A heavenly combination of Paul Sebastian or something sexy like that. I gently get onto the tips of my toes, looking up at him, straight into the windows to his soul, and give him a soft kiss on the lips. The sticky sweet taste Bailey's blends divinely with his lips and I can't help myself. I kiss him once more, this time, sucking the life out of him. I ran out of batteries for my silver bullet, and Shawn has got me hot as hell. Everything on my body aches in anticipation of him. My knees are weak and my clit is swollen. A slight smile escapes his lips, and his warm breath penetrates my nostrils, with the smell of Bailey's. Licking my lip-gloss off of his lips turns me on something serious, and I can't help but make my desires known.

Still near his luscious lips, I inch in closer to him. "Whenever you're ready, Shawn, I'll be here waiting."

He exhales, which signals to me that he may be ready sooner than he thinks. Struggling to get the words out, he manages, "Okay, I'll keep that in mind," as he swallows hard.

I glance briefly at the rising bulge coming from the crotch of his slacks, his dick is growing longer and stronger right before my eyes, and I know he's ready now. I don't want to push it, but I can't help myself. Curiosity killed the cat, but satisfaction can bring this kitty cat back.

Moving in again to kiss him once more, I land another soft peck on his lips, and gently brush his crotch with my hand, and his hot breath escapes his lips once more. "I think you should go now, Shawn. I'm not that strong." I back away from him and head back into the living room.

He approaches me from behind, and whispers in my ear. "I just don't want to get into anything right now. It's been awhile since I've been intimate with someone."

I'm fucking with him now.

Seductively, I walk away from him, grab his coat and hand it to him. We both walk to the front door of my apartment. Leaning in again, I kiss him on his lips, but this time, I lick his lips, then allow my tongue to glide down his chin, onto his neck, gradually coming back to his lips, I kiss him once more as I open the door.

"I had a wonderful time this evening, Shawn. Thank you so much."

"You're quite welcome, Summer."

After I close the door behind him, I press my back against the door, exhaling and inhaling deeply, trying to extinguish the roaring flames that now consume me whole. Removing my blouse and skirt, I leave them right there on the floor, and turn around to lock the door, when the sound of my doorbell scares the living hell out of me. Now in bra and panties only, I lock the door hurriedly, and look through the peephole. Oh it's just Shawn, he must've forgotten something.

"One second, Shawn."

I crack the door, just peeping my head out a little to see if he is okay.

"Everything okay?"

"No." He pushes the door open. I move backwards as he moves in closer to me. Taking his hand, he reaches behind and locks the door then zooms into me rapidly, grabbing my waist, his tongue lands in my mouth with force, hot breath lands across the side of my face, he's hungry. It's been awhile. Lifting me off my feet in a forward pushing movement, we end up near the sofa, where he bends me over, and rips my panties off. I've never had my ass bitten and licked so good in my life.

His tongue travels up the small of my back, like a slithering snake, trying to locate his prey. And I am his prey tonight. Pressing his throbbing, hard rod against my ass, I feel Shawn's thickness and my clitoris responds with huge throbs, along with my walls, which ache in anticipation of what's to come, literally and figuratively.

Turning around, I place my arms around his neck, and return a passionate kiss. Our tongues intertwine, saliva running down the sides of our mouths. He puts his fingers into my mouth, and I suck on them one by one.

"Oh, Summer. I can't hold back anymore." He removes his shirt and exposes a chocolate-coated six-pack. Fuck it. I have to suck his dick.

Dropping to my knees, in pure ecstasy, I unzip his slacks, and they fall to the floor. Pulling down his boxers, those fall to the floor too, leaving only a ten-inch, brown sugar coated rod that commands my attention, wanting and needing my luscious lips around it, making its acquaintance. My tongue slowly creeps out of my mouth, slithering and licking the pre-come, creating a drooling effect, smearing onto my glossy lips, turning Shawn on in the worst way. I glide down the sides of his swelling manhood with my tongue, and admire how it continues to grow as I take it in, head on.

"Oh, Summer. Please, you're going to make me release too soon," he pleads as he strokes the curls of my hair. His rod tickles the back of my throat, and I almost want to gag, but I have to remain smooth and suck this dick like my life depends on it. My head bobs up and down as I stroke him with my tongue, and powerful thrusts in and out of the hot, wet cave I've created for him, takes him to higher plains.

"Oooh," he cooed, while my mouth still clutches firmly around the growing mushroom-headed cock, sucking Shawn into a state of euphoria. A volcanic eruption released from Shawn, as hot semen landed in the back of my throat, and onto my lips, as I swallowed him whole, allowing him a strong orgasm, one that he truly needed.

In a deep, satisfied breath, Shawn expelled, "I'm sorry. It's been a minute. You look so good...your lips, damn, Summer..."

I interrupt him. "I love how you felt in my mouth, the taste of your sweet dick is so good. I've been wanting to taste you for so long, Shawn." I get up and head to the bathroom. Bringing back a washcloth, I walk over to Shawn who is now enjoying a glass of Bailey's, in his boxers only. I clean him, and peck him on the lips. "Sorry if I forced it."

Returning my kiss, he tells me, "No, I loved it. And I hope I can return the favor and give you some pleasure."

I back up. "Anytime, Shawn. Why don't you stay the night? I'm sure you'll be able to think of something over the next few hours." I wave my index finger, motioning him to come to me, and like an obedient puppy, he places his now finished glass of Bailey's onto the table and follows me into my bedroom.

I remove my bra, and walk closer to Shawn. Removing his boxers, and the anticipation of what's to come, has made him solid as a rock, and me, flowing like the Nile River. Laying down on my back, I pull Shawn down on top of me. Reaching down, I grab the head of his dick and rub the pre-come into the tip.

"Damn, Summer." I stroke it gently. "Let me eat your pussy first." He tries to get up.

"We have time for that. I want to feel you deep inside of me, Shawn. Right here, right now. Please."

With one blunt forceful impact, Shawn is inside of me, and his manhood is so thick and long, hitting all of my walls with blatant intent, forcing an immediate orgasm from me upon entry. I'm slowly loosing my mind, lost in lust and desire for this man, I hope will soon be all mine.

"Oh God, Shawn!"

He places his tongue into my mouth, with heavy breath he tells me, "Hush. Let me make you feel good."

As Shawn fucks me, face-to-face, I can feel all that he has to offer. Grabbing his ass cheeks, I bite on his bottom lip, and beg that he fucks me slow and hard. "Shawn, please take your time. I want to feel every inch of your good dick."

His head tilts back, he closes his eyes, only to open them to a serious fuck face, and tells me as he licks his lips, "Anything you want, Summer."

Steering him in and out of my slick, wet cave, is like pulling a knife in and out of a jar of peanut butter, thick, hot and sticky.

Have mercy, he's hitting my spot in the worst way. Unapologetically, he ambushes my pussy, relentlessly, over and over again, forcing multiple orgasms to secrete, draining the life and sense out of me. As my juice flows down his shaft, and onto his sack, he bites my neck, sucking on it with so much intensity. "Your pussy is so juicy, Summer. I love it," he whispers.

If he hits my G-spot with any more force, I'm going to cry. Shit, he feels amazing. I'm about to lose it again. "Shit, Shawn... damn, baby...you feel so fucking good, baby."

Exhaling, digging deeper, penetrating the depths of my soul, Shawn barely gets it out. "You're fucking my head up, Summer."

It's the morning after, and what a sweet morning it is. My cozy bed feels extra warm, as I glide my foot along Shawn's calf. The more I rub, the closer he gets. Hugging me from behind, Shawn's powerful body draws me nearer to him. He's spooning me, and I can feel his hot breath on the back of my neck, as he awakes. I turn my head slightly, to get a glimpse of what he looks like first thing in the morning. Not bad, as I didn't know what to expect. His hold of me is so strong, and wow, his skin is so warm and soft. We're playing "footsies" like two lovebirds. Whispering in my ear, "I can't believe you're single," as he nibbles on my earlobe. "Well, good morning to you too, Mr. Fontaine."

"Good morning. Thank you for last night." Shawn hugs me and then kisses the back of my neck. "You're welcome."

I slither my way from his massive embrace, turn around and prop the pillows behind him.

He leans up, bare-chested and looking sinful. "Where are you going, Summer?"

I hand him the remote to the flat screen. With a flirtatious over the shoulder look, I tell him, "I'm going to make my King breakfast."

"Thank you, my Queen."

Amber
Baby Mama Drama

Finally, we arrive at Shayla's house. I can't believe I actually suggested Khalil's daughter, Lexis, come to Jersey with us for Thanksgiving. He's so adamant about keeping his family together, and so focused on being a real man, that I felt it my wifely duty to jump in and add my two cents. Although I have to admit, I'm a little nervous because I haven't seen Shayla since our college days. I haven't seen Lexis either, since she was born. As I take a quick glance in Khalil's direction, I wonder if he's told her I'm pregnant. It's strange; he doesn't seem nervous at all. Suddenly, I feel like I should've stayed home. The only reason I agreed to come is because Khalil insisted. He's changed so much that it's almost scary. Anything I want, anything I need, he makes sure I get it. I know it has a lot to do with me being pregnant, as he recently discovered, also because he's been a dog, but he's suffocating me.

I tried like hell to get out of this trip, but he wouldn't allow it. He said he wasn't comfortable with me staying home alone and wouldn't be able to forgive himself if something happened to me. I couldn't even persuade him that it would only be for one night and I'd stay with my parents until he got back. He made it very clear and was extremely unwavering about me coming with him. It's funny; he wasn't this persistent a few months ago, not about our love, or marriage.

When Khalil's done parking the truck, I adjust my seat to the upright position and cross my legs. I look down at my wedding ring and begin toying with it. Khalil obviously senses something's wrong because he leans over and gives me a soft kiss on my forehead.

"Amber are you alright?" A look of concern consumes his face.

"I'm okay." I try hard to smile. "Just feeling a little nauseous, that's all. I think I've been in this car too long."

"Do you need anything?" Khalil is being so attentive.. "You wanna go get something to eat before we go in?"

"No, K," I assure him, "I'll be okay. Just need to stretch my legs and get some air, that's all."

"You sure?" Khalil, being his persistent self, rests his hand on my very slightly swollen belly. "There's a store down the street. Maybe you and *my son* could go for a nice cold ginger-ale."

I must admit a cold, ginger-ale sounds inviting, so I give in. "Okay, Khalil." I grin at his implication that I'm having a boy. "Ginger-ale sounds good, but let's walk. I need to get out of this car."

I open the door, but before getting out, I point at the black, tree-shaped air freshener hanging from the rear view mirror. Funny how I would notice something so insignificant.

"And maybe on the way home you could get rid of this air freshener please?"

"That's black ice, baby." Khalil, already removing it, says, "I thought you liked it."

"I did, Khalil." I climb out of the truck. "But now it's sickening. Just thinking about it makes me wanna puke. I pray to God I don't ever have to smell that again for as long as I live."

Khalil smiles and a light chuckle escapes him.

I wonder to myself how something a person can love all their life can all of a sudden become repulsing to them. I used to love black ice, but now that I'm pregnant, my senses are out of whack. Not to mention my nerves are shot, and my tolerance level is at an all time low. I don't know why, but I feel like smacking the shit out of Khalil right now. I actually feel like balling up my fist, and he hasn't done anything wrong. *What the fuck is wrong with me?*

When we step from the car, I realize how cold it is, so I zip up my whiskey-colored fur. Actually, it's a waist length fox Khalil bought me for my birthday. I love the way the fur slides through my fingers when I touch it. I was so surprised when he walked in the house with it that day. He said he saw me looking at it in a magazine so he thought he'd surprise me with it. I really was surprised and I showed him how much later on that night.

Khalil says something that I obviously don't pay attention to and points out Shayla's house as we walk past. I can't help but fantasize while he's talking. Just a second ago, I wanted to connect the dots on his face with my fist. But right now, he's turning me on, in the worst way. I mean turning me on, like he somehow managed to set fire to my loins in the last couple of seconds. The way his freshly trimmed goatee sits atop his mahogany brown skin, reminds me why I managed to stay with him this long. His crisp, black Rockafella jeans loosely sculpt his long, strong thighs. The North Face jacket, same color as my fur, precisely matches his Timberlands. His tasty, full grown lips, perfectly chiseled face, gorgeous teeth, all atop his NBA-like stature, all dipped in ebony, makes my inner thighs quiver just a bit. It's not surprising though, especially since Khalil is always dressed to impress. I just wish he knew that right now he's aiding and abetting my quest for sexual gratification. The other night, Khalil put it on me something serious. I break into a cold sweat, just thinking about how satisfied he left me. I smile as I think about jumping his bones right here on the street. And, I must say, we do look good together.

"What are you smiling about?" With curiosity, Khalil wraps his arm around my neck.

"Nothing," I lie. "I was just thinking about our college days, that's all." I quickly change the subject back to Shayla's house and wonder to myself how someone would even attempt to raise a child in an area like the one she was in before, but I keep my comments to myself. My father always told me if I didn't have anything nice to say, don't say anything at all. Thank goodness, Khalil gave her the money to move, and even assisted with the move. Thank God, she didn't spend the money on bullshit, which was a surprise. Can't take the ghetto out of the trick.

We continue toward the store, all the while, Khalil's holding my hand. I smile and hold onto him tighter than usual. He's turning me on in the worst way and doesn't even know it. He's so protective of me now. He cooks for me, cleans for me and does the grocery shopping. He opens doors, helps me out of bed, and helps me get dressed in the mornings and at night. He irons my clothes, drives me to work and picks me up. He says he doesn't want me driving while I'm pregnant. I told him that's ridiculous but he insists. He's even gone as far as implying I quit my job. He says he wants me to let him be *the man*. Well, needless to say, the conversation didn't last too long because I wasn't having it. I had to remind him I love my work. It attributes to my sanity, so to speak. Keisha's there, my patients are there and it gives me a sense of pride to be able to bring something to the table in our relationship. Khalil hasn't brought it up since.

Once inside the store, I walk directly toward the beverages. Removing two ginger ales, and proceeding to the counter, I look around for Khalil and notice he's in the rear of the store. I walk to the back and find him picking up all sorts of things: fruit, cookies, cereal, milk and more soda.

"Khalil, what are you doing?" I'm growing frustrated because he appears to be buying the entire store.

"Nothing, baby. I just figured I'd get a few things to munch on for the night. Room service prices are ridiculous and I know we're going to get hungry." He does have a point so I allow him to continue shopping. I walk back to the front of the store and tell the attendant to charge Khalil for my soda. I walk outside and figure I'll call Keisha while I wait. She's at work right now, but I know she'll never be caught dead without her cell. I dial Keisha's number and she picks up on the first ring.

"Gurrrl, I been waitin' for you to call!" Keisha exclaims, before I can get a word in. Of course, she has my number programmed with my very own ring tone to boot. "You okay? What that bitch talkin' about? You need me to come down there?"

"Would you shut up, Keisha!" I laugh and proceed. "I'm fine and we didn't even get to Shayla's yet. I mean, we're here but we stopped at the store first. Calm down, girl!" I gotta admit Keisha's been a bit overprotective of me as well since the pregnancy. But then again, she always is when it comes to Shayla.

"Oh, okay." Keisha slows down, becoming less hyper. "Just let me know and I'll gas up the jag with the quickness!"

"Trust me, Keisha, that won't be necessary," I assure her. "I just called to let you know we got here safely. Are you at work?"

"Unfortunately, yeah girl, I'm here." Keisha sounds disgusted.

"How's Mrs. Sampson doing?" I laugh and figure I'll ask about Keisha's newest patient. She's always got a story to tell about this seventy-year-old woman and I could use a good laugh right now.

"Oh, that drunk bitch? That bitch done been through three nurse's assistants today and it's only ten o' clock in the fucking morning. Keeps on coming out here to the desk with these complaints, asking for a new nurse to clean her and help her to the bathroom. Then the wrinkled faced bitch got mad at me 'cause I wouldn't change nurse's for her so she goes back in her room and shits on herself."

"No she didn't, Keisha!"

"Oh yes that bitch did, and guess what?"

"What?" I'm hanging on to Keisha's every word and curious to know what she's done to the poor woman.

"That drunk bitch still layin' in it!" Keisha laughs. "It's been an hour and she's still slippin' and slidin' back there. I bet you she won't shit on herself no fuckin' more. Especially while I'm on duty 'cause from now on, she'll be an itchy ass before I take my black ass back there and clean her up!"

I laugh so hard I almost spill my soda. "So, how's Dr. Peshine?" I ask with a sneaky-ass voice.

"Oh, he's still here, still has jungle fever, still white as you, and still lookin' tempting. We'll talk about that later, girlie."

Khalil emerges from the store so, between laughs, I manage to tell Keisha that I'll call her later.

"What's so funny, Mrs. Devereaux?" Khalil begins to smile himself. "And who are you talking to?"

"That was Keisha," I manage to say, still trying to regain my composure. "She was just telling me about one of the patients."

"What has that crazy ass girl done this time?" Khalil laughs. "See, she's a perfect example of why I'll never put my mother in a home. Keisha's the type of person I'd have to murder in cold blood."

Both of us continue laughing all the way back to Shayla's house. It doesn't even dawn on me that Shayla is standing on her porch. The sight of her startles me and abruptly stops my laughter. Shayla hasn't changed much and, as much as I hate to admit it, she's still a very pretty young woman.

"What the fuck is she doing here, Khalil?" Shayla, with a pouting disappointing look on her face, points at me like I'm the plague.

Khalil releases my hand and walks up on the porch toward Shayla. The look on his face says he means business and the scowl in his eyes co-signs as much. "Look Shayla!" Khalil's voice reaches a high, rough crescendo, as he points in my direction. "We've been over this too many times! Amber is my wife and wherever I go, she has the right to be there as well so, get over yourself!"

It takes everything inside me not to stick out my tongue at Shayla and tease, and yell, "*naaa naaa na naaa naaa.*"

"Muthafucka, this is my house! And you brought that apple-headed bitch down here to my house?" Shayla, like the hood rat she is, is moving her neck side to side and her hands flailing every which way. "She ain't got no fuckin' rights over here! Ain't it enough that you married the bitch? Now you gotta rub it in my face by bringin' her where the fuck me and my daughter live? Nigga you done bumped yo' fuckin' head!"

Okay, enough is enough. I had nothing to do with Khalil dumping her. She knew we were involved when she went after him and now it's my fault. Now I'm the bitch. *Aww, hell no! Pregnant or not, here I come!*

"Shayla, I'd appreciate it if you'd refrain from referring to me with obscenities." I'm hoping we can remain civilized. "I don't disrespect you and I'd like the same consideration in return."

Shayla walks down the stairs, aiming in my direction, nostrils flaring, looking like she's ready to slit my throat. "Bitch, was I talkin' to you?" Shayla spits in my direction and rolls her eyes. "Dis between me and K! You ain't got shit to do wit nuthin'!" The sound of her calling Khalil "K" bothers me more than her calling me a bitch. And if she wants a fight, she's got the right one today. Right now, I can readily identify with Mike Tyson when he bit that son-of-a-bitch's ear off. With frustration, I remove my fur and throw it forcefully to the ground.

"Well guess what, bitch, I'm here and I'm not going any fucking where!" I spew and walk towards Shayla, with aggressiveness. "Bring your skank ass down off that porch and I'll show you just how involved I really am!" Before I can get within two feet of Shayla, Khalil intervenes and grabs me by the arm.

"Amber, are you crazy?" Khalil 's voice is stern. "Have you forgotten you're pregnant? You really think I'll allow you to risk a miscarriage behind Shayla's bullshit?" Khalil picks up my coat, puts it back on me and seethes with anger. "Get in the truck, Amber!"

"Pregnant?" Shayla yells, with pure and uncut venom in her eyes. "I know fuckin' well this bitch ain't pregnant!"

I suddenly realize Khalil hadn't told her. A smile comes over me as I purposely look in Shayla's direction and rub my belly before climbing into the passenger's seat. I also realize how juvenile I'm being at the moment, but then again, look at who I'm dealing with; an angry, bitter, gutter-ass-rat-skank-slut-bitch, who fucked my man and is now blaming me because he didn't choose her. I know I shouldn't refer to another black woman as any of these things, but fuck it! I'm sick and tired of being the better person. I'm sick and tired of being the one who walks away, the one who turns the other cheek, the one who has to be the epitome of class. I'm sick and tired of being good, little Amber! I'm mad as hell right now; at Shayla for disrespecting me this way, and at Khalil for even involving me in this mess. I didn't ask for any of this! No one told him to go off and fuck her. No one told him to get her pregnant. I didn't ask for any of this bullshit, but yet, and still, here the fuck I am! Caught up in these stupid motherfucker's love triangle! I *swear to God* I don't need this shit!

"Khalil, give me the fucking keys!" I yell at him through the car window. He can stay and argue with her for all I care, but I'll be damned if I'm going to sit here and watch!

"Just hold up a sec, Amber." Khalil holds up one finger. "Let me get Lexis and we're outta here, okay?"

"Get Lexis?" I ask, growing angrier by the moment. "You're standing there arguing with her as if I'm not even here and I haven't once heard either of you mention anything about Lexis! Stupid ass bitches! Now give me the fucking keys!" Khalil comes over to the truck and begins explaining to me but I don't wanna hear it.

"Amber, listen baby." Khalil's tone is soft. "I'm sorry if you feel disrespected right now. That wasn't my intention at all. But don't think for a minute that I'm gonna let you fight out here in the street. Do you honestly believe I'd ever allow that to happen? What kind of man would that make me, Amber? You're my wife and you're carrying my baby. You think I'd allow someone like Shayla to interrupt what we have?"

"I can't answer that, Khalil." Frowning, I stare deep into his eyes, because I can't believe he is asking me some shit like this.. "At one point, you *were* fucking her, so exactly what kind of man does that make you? Answer that Khalil. Or should I say, *K*? What does that have to say about *you*?"

Khalil backs up, turns around and walks back to Shayla, like a sorry-ass mutt with his tail between his legs. I'm sorry for my last comment, but I think he needed to hear it. And I know I'm right! Did he suddenly forget that Shayla is the same triflin' ass bitch who schemed on him, Shawn and me by using her sister to break up my marriage? To ruin our lives? Oh shit, I'm laughing out loud. I still can't believe the shit even happened. Can't believe any of that shit happened. Yeah, I look down at my belly as my seed grows. *Yeah, I can't believe any of that shit happened...*

Amber
Turkey Shirts

Look at my baby, in his complete and utter glory. He's holding my hand so tight, I can feel the blood draining out of the left side of my body. Who can blame him? He's excited about his newfound fatherhood. He's finally becoming a real man, and stepping up to the plate, taking care of his daughter Lexis, who is in the back seat of the H2, in her glory as well. Khalil's proud smile makes me happy for him, and, to be honest, I am very proud of him too. Ain't nothing like personal growth, because when you're whole on the inside, it is reflected in all that you do.

Turning around to check on Lexis, I thank God for allowing me to get past my own inner turmoil and to accept Khalil's child. After all, she will have a sibling soon, I pray, so I had to step up my game too. She's a cutie pie too, with cornrows for days, and the cutest dimples I've ever seen. She doesn't look like Khalil, to me anyway, but she damn sure looks like her devil of a mother.

"Are you okay, Lexis?"

"Yes, Amber, I am great."

"Are you excited to see your grandma?"

"Yep."

"Good, I'm sure your grandma is excited about seeing you too."

This Thanksgiving will prove to be a classic as we are headed to Khalil's mom's house to celebrate this year. He wanted to have a family-oriented day, with both his wife and his daughter,

mother, sister and all of his family. Although I really ain't beat
for none of this shit, especially his momz, I couldn't refuse the
opportunity to see Khalil at his best. I want him to enjoy his
family and his daughter. Wow, I've come a long way.

"So, Lexis, what would you like to do this weekend?"

"I don't know, Amber. Maybe we can go to the movies."

"Sounds good to me, but I was thinking we can go and get
our nails and feet done too. Have a girl's day out. How does that
sound to you?"

Her eyes light up and look like dark brown silver dollars.
Her radiant smile can warm anyone's soul. "Wow! That sounds
great, Amber! Daddy, please can we do it?"

Khalil's smile is equally as radiant, but he alarms me a bit,
as he turns around to look at Lexis, while we're on the parkway.
I think he should get back to driving.

"Anything you want, Baby! You and Amber can do that,
and when you're done, I'll be taking my two favorite girls out to
dinner. Lexis, have you ever been to the Olive Garden?"

"No, daddy. But mommy said Malik was going to take us,
but he never did."

"Okay, well we will go this weekend."

"Thank you, daddy."

Khalil's cell phone rings and he activates his blue tooth,
and answers. "What's up?" A few seconds pass, and his smile
reappears. "Happy Thanksgiving to you too, brother."

I glance over to him. He looks at me and smiles. "Yeah,
she's right here. She's here too. They are both good. Can't wait
to see you, brother. Okay, I'll holla."

Khalil takes my hand into his again, now driving with only
one hand, as we approach his mother's house. He pulls my hand
up to his mouth and plants an endearing kiss. Khalil still has the
ability to turn me on with the slightest touch.

"Who was that, baby?"

"Oh, that was Shawn. He said Happy Thanksgiving to you and Lexis. We will see him soon at dinner."

"Will we?"

"Yep, I think on Sunday. We're going out. Mom will watch Lexis. Tell Keisha to come."

"Okay, I will."

Goose bumps take hostage of my arms, as Khalil tells me about our upcoming get together. I haven't seen Shawn in a while so I'm just a bit nervous.

A beautiful, sun-filled chilly day greets us as we park outside of Khalil's mom's house. As Khalil walks over, looking good as all hell, I might add, wearing a pair of black Phat Farm jeans, crisp and clean, with a black turtleneck, and a dark brown, leather jacket, as his brown Perry Ellis boots, offsets it all. The brown skully covering his smooth and clean baldhead gives him a model look today, like he just stepped off the catwalk, from an urban fashion show. As he heads toward me, he smiles, staring deep into my eyes. He's so sweet, and he's trying so very hard. Opening the door for me, he takes me by the hand and helps me out of the truck, and on to the sidewalk.

"K, I'm okay, baby."

"Okay, sweetie, just making sure you're alright."

We both head to the back door, and Khalil opens it for his baby girl. She darts out of the truck, and jumps right into Khalil's arms. Her tiny arms, grab hold of his neck, and she plants the most endearing kiss on his cheek, and smiles. "Thank you, daddy."

It's enough to make a grown man cry as I see Khalil welling up just a bit.

Khalil kisses Lexis on her cheek, and puts her on his hip. She clutches on for dear life, arms still hugging his neck. Khalil takes my hand, and we walk up the stairs to once again, visit the Thunderdome.

Considering that Khalil's hands are full at the moment, between Lexis and holding on to me for dear life, I ring the doorbell. Immediately after I press it, the front door flies open and there's Kiana, who grabs Lexis right out of Khalil's arms. Sporting her Thanksgiving wear, Kiana has on a white tee shirt, with a turkey on it, but not just any turkey, it is an African American inspired turkey, as it has on fashionable bling around its neck, and in style sneakers on its feet, and in quotation marks next to its mouth are the words, "Happy Thanksgiving, you jive turkey."

Never in my life have I witnessed something this ghetto. But that's not it. Khaki-colored Capris, with turkey ornaments throughout, match the tee shirt, and also correspond with the tan-colored flip flop sandals, which are open-toed, exposing Kiana's need to have ten pedicures, and the thick red toenail polish is chipped on every thick nail, and does not match her dark brown skin at all. Her toenails have to be about three inches long, and if I don't stop staring, I will heave, right now. My eyes quickly go in the opposite direction, scrolling back up her very tiny, crackhead frame, and now notice, chickenhead, Doublemint twins, as Whiteboy, Kiana's love, has on matching tee shirt, and matching khaki pants. However, no matching flip slop sandals, and for that, I am so very grateful. Instead, Whiteboy chose dirty red and white high top Pro Ked sneakers. I'm assuming he's going for an old Larry Bird look. My eyes scan further up, with all focus now on Whiteboy, who smiles at me, and gives me a bird's eye view of his greenish, yellow teeth, the kind only a crackhead could adorn. And his thick ass Coke bottle frames, makes his eyes look like tiny little beads, making the name beady-eyed chickenhead so befitting for the sight I now behold. A wet, dog haired shag haircut or lack there of, completes Ebony and Ivory, as this pair could easily star in a twenty-first century version of The Adams Family. Also running to the front door are Candelabra and Chandelier, Candy and Chandy for short, Whiteboy and Kiana's twin girls. Now, unless I'm really mistaken, as dark as these two little fat Buddhas are, they are in no way, shape or form, Whiteboy's biological children. It's simply impossible.

Grabbing my hand, Whiteboy pulls me into the house and Kiana gives me a big kiss on my cheek, which again, makes me want to splatter my breakfast all over the floor, as I know for damn sure, Kiana ain't brushed her teeth since the last time I saw her, which was at my wedding.

"Amber, you look good, girl," she screams as Whiteboy pulls me further into the house.

The dust bunnies aligning the curtains look like they actually came with the curtains, thick and white, and screaming allergic reaction. I see not much has changed in the Thunderdome, unless, of course, you add in the turkey ornaments and Thanksgiving designs strategically placed in the living room.

"Thanks, Kiana. You look very festive today. All nice and Thanksgiving like."

"Girl, you ain't said nothing but a word, 'cause I got you and Khalil, and my niece, tee shirts just like this one, for today." She signals to Whiteboy with the waving of her hand. We won't get into her chipped red fingernails, which spell welfare and food stamps. She puts Lexis down. Poor child looks scared, and I don't blame her. Kiana bends down to give Lexis a kiss on the cheek and Lexis grabs onto Khalil's leg. "Awe, ain't she darlin', Khalil. I'm gonna cry. She is so sweet." She signals for

Whiteboy again and screams, "Whiteboy! Bring me the turkey shirts for Amber and them."

Whiteboy rushes over with the tee shirts, hands them to Kiana, and makes himself clear, with a slurred voice, like he just shot up a day's worth of horse tranquilizers. "Okay, Kiana. But don't be yellin' at me," he says, in a slow slur, eyes half closed. *A mind is a terrible thing to waste.*

A loud boom rocks the floor, and an equally loud Bigfoot enters the room. Weighing in at a masculine three hundred pounds, with equally powerful beard, and size twelve feet, is none other than, drum roll please, "Momz!" Khalil's mother steps into the living room to greet us all, moves in close to Lexis, and tries to snatch her, but she holds onto Khalil's leg for dear life, and screams, "Daddy!" Khalil reassures Lex that the monster doesn't want to eat her, rather its her grandma wanting to say "Hi."

Khalil bends down and pries Lexis off of his leg. "It's okay, Lexis. This is grandma Athena." Lexis looks up at her daddy, puts her hand on her hip, and points to Mrs. Devereaux, her grandma, and says, "That's a man, daddy. Where's my grandma?"

Momz leans in and grabs Lexis, and lifts her. "I'm grandma, Lex," she says as she kisses her on the cheek.

"Oh." Lexis smiles and hugs her grandma, at the same time looking at her dad like she wants to cry. Mrs. Devereaux looks me up and down, and barely says a word.

I smile, knowing that you catch more flies and dinosaurs with honey. "Happy Thanksgiving, Mrs. Devereaux." I kiss her on the cheek.

She looks at Khalil. "So, you gonna have another light-skin chile, huh, Khalil?"

Khalil smiles, like that was really a compliment. "Yes, mom, get ready for another grandchild." He moves close to me, and rubs my belly. "My son will be here soon."

I smile again because Khalil swears we're having a boy.

"Well, ain't y'all gonna put your turkey shirts on? We gotta get ready for Thanksgiving dinner." Kiana hands us all a tee shirt to put on. I head into the bathroom and put on my tee shirt, folding up my silk blouse and placing it into my handbag. Kiana could get about twenty bucks for this shirt, and I'm sure Khalil paid about one hundred for it. As I head out of the bathroom, Lexis is standing there, and I pull her into the bathroom with me to change her clothes.

She looks up at me. "Amber, I love you," she confesses and hugs me dearly.

"I love you, too, Lexis and I am so happy that you are visiting us this week."

"I wish I could stay with you forever, Amber."

As I remove her shirt, I notice a few marks on Lexis' back that make me uncomfortable. I run my fingers slightly across the purple-colored, two-inch markings. "Does that hurt, Lexis?" I ask as she tries to put her shirt back on.

"No, Amber. I'm okay. I fell when I was riding my bike."

No way in hell do I believe her, but I am not going to upset the day, so I will readdress the issue later on. I help Lexis change her shirt, and now she is matching me, in her turkey shirt. What a day this will be. I'm alarmed by what I just saw, and need to figure out a way to tell Khalil. Somehow, the love I've started to feel for this little girl, has multiplied within a matter of seconds, and I now feel the need to keep her safe and protected.

We walk out of the bathroom and a cheesy ass grin crosses my face as I see Khalil, sitting at the dining room table, in his turkey tee, looking handsome and ghetto fabulous at the same

time. Big Momma Bird, I mean Momz, is back and forth from
the kitchen to the dining room table, bringing out big bowls,
which contain our delicious dishes of dinner. Dollar store turkey
inspired bowls, hold those goddamn make-you-shit–all-day-and-
night collard greens, sweet potatoes which seem to have the skins
still on parts of them, macaroni and cheese, which looks like
single wrapped slices of cheese was melted on top, along with
an overdose of paprika for coloring, and turkey, damn turkey,
dressed with carrots all around, and fancy beading throughout.
I think she's been watching the Food Network too much and
has failed at mimicking what she sees. Thank goodness, I'll be
stopping at my parent's on the way home, where I can really
throw down. I'm hungry and the baby is hungry, but ain't no
way in hell, I'm eating any of this shit.

ꙮ ꙮ ꙮ

Well, things don't go exactly as planned, as I've been here
four hours longer than I expected. In addition, my eyes are
watering, my nose is itchy, I guess from the lack of fresh air
and vacuuming, and my stomach is cramping, aching, hurting
so bad, I guess from the dirt-filled greens, or from the bloodshot
turkey I consumed. Having believed the myth that all black
women can cook, I once again was fooled and succumbed, and
this time, I'm really gonna pay for it. I'm not that far along with
the pregnancy, but my child ain't used to this and the flutters in
my belly confirm as much.

Wow, here comes dessert. No wonder Khalil loves my
cooking so much. I wondered over the years why he was so
adamant about me staying in the kitchen, but I wonder no more,
as the tray of banana pudding lands at the center of the table. The
bananas lay across the top in a way I'd never seen prior to today.

My mom taught me to make banana pudding with French vanilla pudding, bananas and Nilla wafers. I throw my little special touches here and there, but that's the basis for a good pudding. This shit right here, is some shit right here, for lack of a better description. Brown-edged banana slices, across cookies, actual fucking cookies, not Nilla wafers, but dollar store, cheap ass artery clogging, third world country cookies. Whipped cream, I guess has taken place of actual pudding, and I laugh out loud. Fuck it. If Khalil decides to divorce me, then so be it, but I ain't holding this shit in any longer. I'm already going to be on the toilet all damn night, so I deserve this moment.

Keisha
European Inspired

W ho were you talking to, Keisha? I thought you were only into me tonight."

"Oh, Greg, I am only into you tonight. And, I thank you for a loving evening. I've never had Thanksgiving dinner on a dinner cruise before."

Taking a walk back to our table, after almost an hour on the dance floor, Dr. Peshine grabs my hand and leads the way. This is luxury, and splendor at its finest. A European-inspired evening, via Dr. Peshine's white ass, as well as the cuisine on New York's Harbor cruise; I'm in awe and on my best behavior tonight. I am on the arm of a fine ass doctor and I'm loving every minute of the New York skyline as it spreads before us in all directions. The gourmet cuisine, fine wines, live jazz and bangin' dance music is serious on this amazing dining cruise—truly an experience as inspiring as the city itself. I'm also inspired by Greg.

All the things that I was teased about as a child, Greg adores. While on the dance floor, he grabbed my ass, as we slow jammed. An eighties soul group, the Dazz Band, appeared out of no where with their version of Norman Connors 1976 *Quiet Storm* classic, *You Are My Starship*. I love that song, and was thrilled and turned on at the same time when it played. Greg held on to me so tight, and sang the words in my ear. I didn't know how or why he would know the words to the song, but I'm glad he did. That's why I had to call Amber.

Blacky, nigger, spook and jiggaboo, were all the words they used to call me growing up. I was fooled, for a long time, believing that my skin was too dark. Everyone equated it to all that was dark and ugly, I had no choice. I never see me, or anyone like me, in the music videos or in the magazines. But Greg, he loves the so-called "wrong" things about me. The only thing holding me back is me. I have to get over the Tom Cruise thing.

He whispered in my ear. "I love your skin. It's so smooth and rich, Keisha."

"Thank you, Greg."

"And, excuse my French, but your ass is unbelievable. I've never seen anything like it up close."

"Ha, ha, you're silly, but thanks."

"Why don't you have a man, Keisha?"

"Well, I'm kind of dating a guy."

"Oh, I remember you telling me that."

"Yeah."

"But, yet and still, you're here with me. Why?"

"I don't know, Greg."

"I think you do know, Keisha. And for the record, I like you too."

"I'm just–"

"Don't explain. You'll eventually let that zero know you've found a hero."

"Huh?"

"Yes, Keisha, I know Doug E. Fresh. You need to get with this hero."

I can replay it over and over again in my mind. We now sit and wait for the waitress to bring us another round of champagne. Greg must've ordered it earlier. He takes my hand.

"Keisha, are you enjoying yourself?"

"Yes, I am." A smile crosses my lips. My ghetto side has taken the night off. I hope nothing brings the Negro out of me.

"Good, because I won't stop until you're mine."

"Is that right?"

"Definitely, Keisha, you are one of the most beautiful women I've ever seen."

"You've got to be kidding me, Greg."

"Why?"

"Because I'm sure you've had the Pam Anderson types."

"And?"

"And, that's what I mean."

"Don't believe the hype."

"What?"

"Yes, Keisha, I listen to Public Enemy too. I like you, dark skin, fat ass, intelligent, strong black woman. If I wanted Pam Anderson tonight, that's who I'd be with."

"I like the sound of that, Greg."

"Good. And, like I said, when you're ready to get rid of this "Jamal" guy, or whatever his name is, let me know. I'm serious about mine, Keisha."

"Ha, ha. You're funny."

"Yeah, well, maybe so, but I know what I like. Now, let's go out on the balcony, enjoy the winter air, and the New York skyline. We'll get our champagne later."

"Sounds good."

Once again, Greg takes me by the hand and leads me up the stairs and out onto the balcony. He's got a nice ass for a white boy, and the way he looks over his shoulder every few seconds to check me out is going to make me wrap my thighs around his neck. Those piercing blue eyes and jet-black hair are an aphrodisiac at this point. He's got good genes, that's for damn sure. Damn, I bet his ancestors are rolling in and out of their fucking graves tonight! Ha, ha, bitches! What!

"What are you wearing, Greg?"

"You mean cologne?"

"Yes."

"Um, it's Giorgio Armani. Do you like?"

"Yes, very nice."

"Keisha, you look so cold. Here come closer to me, I'll keep you warm."

I move in close to Greg and he puts his arm around me. A soft kiss lands on my cheek. "Better?"

"Much."

"What? My warmth or my kiss?"

"Both."

Our eyes connect, and we simultaneously lean in toward each other. The anticipation of his kiss has my coochie tingling. I close my eyes.

The warmth and gentle touch of his soft caress, is a perfect combination to his ultra soft kiss. A small peck, but it was delightful. I open my eyes, to see Greg smiling.

"I've been wanting to do that for a long time, Keisha."

"Really?"

"Why are you so surprised about everything, Keisha?"

"I don't know, Greg. Just never met anyone like you."

"I think it's more than that, Keisha. But, I'm happy to be the one to tell you. You are sexy, and beautiful, Keisha."

"Thank you."

"But, I didn't get a good enough taste of your lips."

"Well, you should try again."

What was once a cheesy Justin Timberlake smile, is now foreplay for me. The touch of his thumb on my cheek, as it brushes softly, is going to make me invite him to the tingle in my spine. Another soft kiss on my lips, and this time he's generous, giving me a sample of his sweet, pink tongue. As I return the favor, my moment of bliss is interrupted by a she-devil.

"Oh shit, bitch! Work it out, now! Well, if it isn't ebony and ivory living together in perfect fucking harmony!"

Ain't this a bitch! Scott's gay ass is here. Well, I ain't that surprised, considering that the stars are out, and he is a twinkle toes. But, damn, who's that next to him? Shit, that brother is fine as wine. Scott's punk ass knows how to pick 'em. Let me keep my composure, because Scott has the ability to bring out the most ignorant coon in me.

"Oh, hi, Scott." I point to Greg. "This is my date, Dr. Gregory Peshine."

"Is that right?" Scott walks toward Greg and circles around him, tugging at the bottom of his jacket, admiring his smoke gray suit. Greg's suit is prepared, cut, constructed and finished completely by hand, and Scott knows it.

"Merino wool?" Scott asks as he rubs the shoulder of Greg's jacket.

Greg appears to be uncomfortable and I'll just explain the shit to him later. I pray Scott doesn't show his ass, because then, I'll have to show my ass, and I just don't want to do that.

"Yes, it is," Greg replies. He looks at me and then back to Scott.

"I see. Exceptional softness and an uncompromising fit."

Greg laughs, and I want to jump off the balcony, straight into the Hudson River. "Yep." Greg laughs out loud.

"So, how do you know Keisha, Dr. Peshine?"

"Scott!" I yell as politely as I can, while rubbing Greg's arm.

"I'm curious as to why a white doctor would want to take out a sister? And, on Thanksgiving at that? That's all."

Damn, I want to die, right now, yep, no matter what. I smile, a big, I'm-gonna-fuck-you-up-later smile, and take Greg by the hand. "Let's go see if our champagne is back, Greg. Good to see you, Scott."

I pull Greg by his arm and he stands firm.

"Wait, Keisha. I want to answer your friend. Well, Scott. I feel like I'm the luckiest man alive tonight. I'm enjoying Thanksgiving dinner with the most sexiest woman I've ever seen in my life. Why do you ask?"

"I ask because, although I normally would call Keisha every black hooker bitch in the book, I can do that, but only me. I want to make sure she's in good hands, because I've been known to make muthafuckas disappear."

Greg pats Scott on the arm. "Well Scott, Keisha is in good hands like All State. And, I plan to try harder than Avis. Why don't you do us a favor and play David Copperfield and disappear this time. Later."

Amber
Truth Hurts

Thanksgiving dinner was, to say the least, interesting. I thank God, as I hadn't laughed so hard in quite some time. Momz is definitely a site to behold, as is her beloved only daughter, Kiana. Ringling Bros ain't got shit on that damn circus. But, what I can't seem to get out of my mind, are the damn tiny figurines strategically placed throughout the house, which seem to have the same gigantic dust balls on them as the God-forsaken curtains. The same curtains that have been hanging in the house since the first time I visited many moons ago. The same curtains that haven't been dusted, washed or changed since Jesus wept.

I see it like this; poor Kiana has three options if she wants to improve her circumstance: kill herself, kill Whiteboy or kill Momz, because someone definitely has gotten a hold of the poor girl's mind, and has ruined her. For her to be so young, she certainly ages rapidly and unapologetically, similar to a white woman.

The sun sets as we are riding home, and my husband still appears to be in his glory. My hand is still clutched in his and he holds on tight. I glance over to him and give him a warm and endearing smile. A smile that tells him I'm proud of him, and I am. He stepped up to the plate and has become such a wonderful man.

I must admit, I'm hungry as hell. I shoved down whatever food I could, without puking right there on the dining room table, but my stomach is growling something awful. And, the baby is fluttering and telling me he's hungry too. Did I say he? Wow, Khalil has definitely rubbed off on me.

We pass Baskin Robbins and Khalil does exactly what I think he's going to do, which is to pull over to get ice cream, and I, for one, am very happy about that. I want to eat one of everything they have in here. Glancing back to check on Lex, I look at her and smile. Her little head is tilted to the side, and she barely has her eyes open. For a girl just turning eight, she is both tiny and sassy, all rolled into one. She's quite adorable.

"Lex, honey, you okay?" I rub her thigh. She stretches, sits up, and smiles while rubbing her eyes. This is Khalil's opportunity to play daddy again, and he loves it.

"Hey, baby. Want some ice cream?"

"Yes, daddy!" Lexis answers sweetly, with eyes as wide as silver dollars.

"Then it's settled. We're getting ice cream." He parks the truck. Turning around to look at Lexis, Khalil whispers, "Don't tell your mom I gave you ice cream this late."

"Mama doesn't let me have ice cream. We never get it, daddy. But I promise, I won't tell," she responds sadly.

How do I tell Khalil about the marks I saw on her? Can I possibly reveal to my husband that his daughter may be suffering from abuse? If there was ever a time I needed to pray, the time is now. I've been saying my silent prayers since I took off her shirt. Praying to God that my eyes were deceiving me and hoping that I was not exaggerating. I've been a nurse too long, so I know the signs of abuse when I see them. But she still has time to be saved. Her soul has not been stripped away, and thank God, she's got a soul. God protects babies and fools. You would never be able to tell this girl lives in the environment she does.

Khalil, once again, walks around the front of the truck, and opens the door for me. He's so sweet. Taking my hand, he helps me out of the H2. "Thanks honey."

"You're welcome, doll." Khalil leans in to peck me on the lips. "And thank you for staying by my side, Amber. You mean the world to me, girl."

We take a step back to open the door for Lex. Khalil has a look of fear on his face as he looks inside the back seat.

"What's wrong, Khalil?"

"Lex is not here. Oh God, Amber!"

"Calm down, K. She was just here!" I frantically push Khalil out of the way, and look in the back seat.

"Surprise!" Lexis jumps up and laughs aloud. I look at Khalil, who looks like he just suffered a stroke, and smile.

He leans in to pick Lexis up and kisses her on the cheek. "Why did you scare daddy like that?"

"I don't know daddy, I was just playing with you." She kisses him on the cheek.

Following the two of them, as we walk into Baskin Robbins, makes me smile, as I admire how tightly Lexis holds on to her dad, and how Khalil, in return, embraces her as she holds on for dear life. This tells me that he will be a good father to our child. It gives me an awesome sense of security.

"Ooh, daddy, can I have that? Ooh and that? And daddy, I want that!" Damn, little mama is pointing to every damn thing in here. What the fuck is Shayla doing down there, running a fucking Nazi camp? Poor girl. I smile as I look at the two of them interact and wonder how in the hell I plan to tell Khalil about his child. God give me strength, because it has to be soon.

As Khalil puts Lexis down, he looks back at me, and smiles. "What are you and my son going to have?"

"K, you so crazy. I think *we* want a banana split. Is that okay?"

"Anything you want, darlin'."

"Oh, K?"

"Yes, baby."

"Have them put some extra hot fudge on there. The baby needs it."

"Is that right?" He smiles at me.

"Yes."

I take a step back towards an empty spot in the ice cream parlor to retrieve my phone. I have no idea who's calling, but it's most likely another Happy Thanksgiving phone call. I look over to Khalil and Lexis again, and notice how she hunches forward, almost leans over, each time Khalil rubs her back. I'm ready to commit murder.

"Hello?"

"Hey, bitch!"

"Hey, Scott, dear Happy Thanksgiving."

"Same to you, baby girl. How are you?"

"I'm good, sweetie. Just in the ice cream parlor with Khalil and Lexis."

"Oh, you got that little bastard with y'all. I can't believe her ghetto mother let her out of the house."

"Well, it was like pulling teeth."

"So, how is the little terror? Is she stank just like her mother?"

"No, Scott, actually, she is a beautiful little darling child. I feel sorry for her."

"I don't blame you honey. Well listen, sweets, let me go. Me and Shaaaaaaannnnne have plans tonight. Kisses."

"Bye, Scott."

After I close my flip, my cell rings immediately. Khalil and Lexis have already taken a seat at a free table and have begun eating. I'm ready to sit my ass down and eat too, so I plan to answer this call really quick and get right into those damn delicious ass bananas. The thought of the hot fudge is making me so anxious. This is the most fun part about being pregnant. I get to eat whatever the hell I want, with a valid excuse.

"Hello?"

"Wassup, bitch?"

"Oh, hey, Keisha. Happy Thanksgiving, sister."

"How you doing, girlie?"

"I'm good, Keisha. We here getting ice cream."

"Who?"

"Me and Khalil and Lexis."

"Oh. How is the little bastard? Is she a handful?"

"No, she's actually a good girl. But, Keisha, we need to talk. She's got some marks on her that ain't right."

"Word?"

"Yes, and I gotta tell Khalil tonight."

"Yeah, you betta. Damn, I'm ready to fuck that bitch up."

"Any who, Keisha. Wassup with you?"

"Girl, I didn't tell you, because I didn't want to hear your big ass mouth. But I went out to dinner with Dr. Peshine for Thanksgiving."

"You did? Keisha you have to tell me all about it!" I yell and smile in response to Keisha's revelation.

"Yes, and guess where I am now?"

"Where?"

"On a boat ride in the city.

"Girl…"

"Amber, we will talk more, but Dr. Peshine, I mean Greg, took me on one of those dinner cruises on the Hudson River. Girl, this shit is so fucking romantic. We circled around New York City. He just went to the bathroom, so I wanted to sneak in a quick call to say Happy Thanksgiving to my best friend."

"Keisha, I can't tell you how excited I am. Oh my God, when I see you, you have to tell me all about it."

"Amber, you know this white boy ain't my cup of tea, but he is definitely not like any brother I've ever been with. He brought me flowers. Picked me up from my home, in a damn Porsche, and paid for everything. Girl, he took me out on the dance floor and held me so tight, whispering them damn sweet little nothings in my ear. Amber, I'm ready to give him some ass."

"Girl, you are crazy. Let's talk more about him tomorrow."

"Okay, girlie. I'll call you tomorrow. Bye."

As I walk over to meet Lexis and Khalil, Lexis gets up and takes me by the hand to my chair. "Come on, Amber, you have to taste this ice cream. It's so good."

"Is it, Lexis?"

"Mmm hmmm."

Khalil smiles a deep dimple pitted smile and looks on proudly as his daughter makes her triple scoop ice cream sundae a distant memory.

ری ری ری

I can barely make it up the stairs of our townhome, from eating the entire banana split. My goodness, did I have to eat the entire thing? I take off my shoes and grab Lexis by her hand and take her up to the bathroom for a bath. "Lex, let's get you ready for your bath, okay? We can watch a movie afterwards."

"Okay, Amber."

"Okay, Lexis. I'm going to get your pajamas out of your room. Which ones do you want?"

"I want the ones you picked out, Amber. The Dora ones."

"Great. I will get those and be right back."

I run the bath for Lexis and add the bubble bath to it. As I head into Lexis' room, I pull out the new pajamas we got her during our trip to the mall. The shit Shayla sent her up here with was a damn shame, to say the very least. Some old, dingy tee shirts for her to sleep in. Come on, now. As Khalil stretches out on the sofa, watching some sports show, I walk back into the bathroom, and see that Lexis has gotten her little ass in the tub. She's adorable.

"You're a big girl, Lexis."

"Yup."

I hang her pajamas up, and prepare her towel and slippers. After doing so, I sit on the edge of the tub and lather Lexis' washcloth. While rubbing her shoulders softly with the cloth, Lex cringes just a bit. With the lighting in the bathroom, I get a clearer visual of the abuse. Some green bruising and purple bruising on her upper and mid back, and whelps on her sides. I slowly move down her back, and can't help but ask, "Does this hurt, Lexis?"

"A little bit." She holds her head down in embarrassment.

I look up and see that Khalil is in the bathroom with us. I see the rage building, and try to calm him, but he's beyond being calmed, as tears stream down his face. "Lex, baby, who did that to you?"

Her head still lowered in embarrassment, she begins to cry, and in a very low audible whisper, she whimpers, "Mama."

I take Lexis out of the tub, dry her off, and help her with her pajamas. "Now, Lex, I want you to go to the living room and we'll get ready for our movie."

"Okay."

As Khalil and I watch Lexis go down the stairs, she skips in delight. Khalil looks at me, tears running down his face. "I ain't sending her back, Amber. I can't send my baby girl back to that type of abuse. I feel like killing that bitch, for using my baby as a fuckin' punchin' bag."

Shayla
Daddy's Little Girl

Hmmmph. What da fuck I'm doin' eatin' fuckin' Thanksgiving Dinner without my baby? I can't believe I let Khalil take my daughter away from me this week. Of all muthafuckin' weeks, he chose a holiday week. Now, I'm sittin' in this fuckin' cramped ass garden apartment lookin' at Lee Lee's ditsy ass, still cryin' over bitch ass Shawn, eatin' turkey and stuffin'.

She over there, lookin' like a fuckin' fool, sitting at the dinette Khalil bought for me and Lex, constantly cryin' over Shawn's miserable, high falutin' ass. I keep tellin' her that any other nigga in the world would love to fuck her ass, but nooooooo, she don't wanna hear that shit. Malik ova there tryin' ta make her dumb ass feel better, huggin' on her and shit. Me and Malik been kickin' it off and on for years now. He a'ight. He ain't Khalil, the bastard. That fuckin' Khalil know he got some good ass dick, and that fat ass, pure white bitch gettin' all of it.

"Lee Lee! Would you shut the fuck up? Damn. Shawn don't want yo' ass. How many times you gon' call his ass?" She lookin' up at me, eyes looked like she been smokin' weed all night. They blood shot. Nose got snot runnin' all down it. Damn, my sister is fucked up. But shit, if Shawn is anything like Khalil's good ass, I see why she cryin'. Dem good ass niggas be hard as hell to find. And, all the goody two shoes bitches be snatchin' 'em with da swiftness. And they betta had, with bitches like me around. I'll snatch yo' nigga up, quick. Shit, how you think me and Malik got together? He used to be my girl's man, but guess what? He mines now. Shit.

"But, Shay, me and Shawn had something good going on! It was you," she points her fragile finger at me, "who ruined my good life. I had a good life with Shawn, Shayla!" Aaliyah yells and cries. Yeah, bitch, cry me a river.

"No, dumb ass, you shoulda kept Shawn. You's the stupid ass that was up there, tryna fuck Amber's fat ass. See, that's what you get for not listenin' to me. If you woulda went up there and tried to fuck Khalil, like I told you, I coulda had my nigga back, and you coulda still been fuckin' Shawn!" I yell back at her silly ass.

"Can't you see, Shayla? There is a better life out there for us. You're acting just like mama. There is so much more to living than taking men for their money and pretending to have their children, Shayla. I mean listen to the way you talk. Your whole thought process is so screwed, Shayla."

No, she didn't!

I walk my fine ass over to Aaliyah, and get right up in her face. See, I knew she was gonna come back here ackin' like she all dat.

"Listen, bitch, you may be my sister and all, but don't think for one minute that yo' ass is betta than me. You hear me? You livin' in my house now, Lee Lee. Why? 'Cause when Shawn kicked your stupid ass out, you ain't have no where ta go. So, enjoy your Thanksgiving dinner with yo' sister, and everything is gon' be alright. 'Kay, Lee Lee?" I gotsta feel sorry for her stupid ass. She ain't got the good sense the Lord gave her.

I sit at the table and begin eating with her. I have to admit that my Thanksgiving dinner is bangin' too. If I don't know how to do nothing else, I damn sure knows how to cook. Shit, when me and K was together, he always had me cookin'. He ate like a fuckin' champ, too—my coochie and my dinner. Ha! I can't stand his black ass, but I love his ass to death. And one day, he gon' be mine, trust.

Lee Lee interrupting our dinner to call Shawn's ass again is pissin' me tha fuck off. Look at her sorry ass. Got da phone to her damn ear, shakin' and feenin like a crackhead.

"Hello, Shawn?" she cryin' hard as hell. "No, Shawn, please, wait. I just wanna say, Happy Thanksgiving to you. Huh? Okay, I love you, Shawn." She starts that damn howlin' again and stares at the phone like Shawn gon' jump out and kiss her.

"What he say, Lee Lee?"

"He said, Happy Thanksgiving."

"Well, that's good."

"No, it's not, Shayla! He said he was having dinner with his girlfriend."

That muthafucka got a new girlfriend? I ain't surprised though. I remember I tried to get a piece of that nigga's good ass dick. He wasn't tryna hear it, though. Said he couldn't and wouldn't do that shit to his boy. I told him nobody would know. He was like, "Shayla, are you out of your mind? You are indeed a beautiful woman, but Khalil is not like a brother, he *is* my brother and I would never sleep with you. Never, Shayla. What you need to do is get some morals."

❧ ❧ ❧

I been callin' Khalil's ass all goddamn day, and he ain't pickin' up his phone. I know my daughter betta be a'ight, dat's for damn sure.

I walk into the kitchen again, and get all of us some more Pepsi. But also grab the fuckin, Crystal Light for Aaliyah's wanna be Tyra Banks ass.

I pour her drink and give her some more tissue, and help her stupid ass blot away her tears. Malik sittin' over there eatin', lookin' like a greedy ass bulldog. Now, I'ma call Khalil back. It's damn nine o'clock. He betta be home with my baby. But this time, I'll call his house. Maybe his phone needs chargin'.

Picking up to dial Khalil's house, I take the phone into my bedroom, and sit down on the bed. I unbutton these tight ass Baby Phat jeans, so I can breathe. Now, why this bitch have to answer the phone?

"Hello, Devereaux residence," that fat ho answers the phone. I swear she sees my number and tries to rub that shit in.

"Put K on da phone," I yell at her fat ass.

"Who's calling?"

"Amber, look, bitch, you know it's me, Shayla."

"Shayla, why are you calling my home and calling me names?"

"Like I said, put K on the phone."

"Don't you mean, Khalil, my husband?"

"Whateva, bitch."

"Well, Shayla, Khalil is in the shower, getting ready to get into our bed. I will have him call you. I'm about to go in there and join him."

I'ma fuckin' kill this hog one day. "Where's my daughter, bitch?"

"Oh, Lexis. My stepdaughter is right here. We were just watching a movie, and having cookies and milk. She is a beautiful child, Shayla. I hope you do right by her."

"Bitch, put my daughter on the phone."

A few seconds pass and Lex is on the phone.

"Hey, mama."

"Hey Lex. How you doin'?"

"I'm good, mama. Me and Amber are watching a movie. Mama, we had so much fun at my grandma's house. We ate Thanksgiving dinner, and then, on the way home, we got ice cream, and then, we got cookies, and then…"

"Okay, baby. You havin' fun?"

"Yup."

"Mama, can I stay another week? Please? Amber is taking me to get my nails and feet done on Saturday, then we are going to the movies, then we are going to the Olive Garden, and Amber said I can order whatever I want, and then…"

"We'll see, Lex. Where's your daddy?"

"Oh, daddy getting out of the shower, mama. Mama, daddy is not a no good bastard like you said. He is so nice, mama. I love him so much, mama. And guess what, mama? I'm gonna have a lil brother or a lil sister!"

"That's nice, Lex."

"And mama. Amber doesn't even yell at me when I do something bad. She told me that we all make mistakes. She hugs me and kisses me, and I even have my own bedroom, mama. Amber and daddy took me shopping and bought me clothes and shoes, and when we went out to lunch, and I spilled the soda on myself. Amber didn't even slap me, mama. I love her so much."

"Lex, okay, damn. Put your father on the phone. You comin' home."

"But no, mama, please, I don't wanna come home, right now." Lexis starts that cryin' bullshit. She lucky she ain't here 'cause I would take that extension cord and light her ass on fire like I did last week.

"Hello?"

"Khalil! Wassup, baby?"

"Shayla! Are you fuckin' crazy? Amber showed me those marks on Lexis, Shayla and the shit ain't cool. Lex ain't coming home until I get this shit checked out."

"What?"

"What, bitch? You heard what I said. *My* daughter ain't coming back down there until I take her to the doctor."

"Khalil!"

"Khalil, nothing, bitch. Let me find out you been beating on my child. I'm going to get sole custody of Lexis and she can live with me and Amber, you triflin' ass cunt. I can't believe you, Shayla. But see, this shit is my fault, and for now on, I will be protecting my child."

"Nigga, ain't nobody been beatin' on her. She always fallin' off her bike, nigga. You know how kids do."

"What the fuck ever, Shayla. Until I get confirmation that my daughter is cool from head to toe, you ain't gotta worry about seeing her. I am getting a lawyer on Monday, and I'm keepin' my child, Shayla."

"Khalil! Amber lyin'. Lex ain't got no marks on her back. Your wife is a fat ass liar, that's all. She just don't want us together, K. She saw how you was lookin' at me when you was down here. She just jealous."

Khalil starts laughin' hard as hell on the other end. "Bitch, you off the chain! Amber? Jealous of your grimy ass? Shit, maybe when you had my nose wide open, but not now. I wish I knew then, what I know now. You ain't nothing but a ho, Shayla. I just couldn't see it back then. Thank God, my wife stayed with me. Now, getting back to you, I never said Lexis had marks on her back, bitch! Now, I know for sure she ain't coming back home to you. I'll see you in court, Shayla."

"Khalil!"

"Bye, bitch."

Click.

Amber
Point of No Return

The crisp, almost winter air is refreshing, and calming this Sunday evening. The moon is shining bright, illuminating the sky, and my life it seems, as I can admit that I am finally coming out of my self-loathing, and starting to appreciate life for what its worth. Khalil's bachelor party fuck up is unforgivable, but the resentment I harbor is only killing me, and I deserve more than that. Not even Khalil can give me what I'm worth, only I can do that.

My spirits have never been more alive. Now that I'm with child, I'm beginning to appreciate, fully, all of the most important things in my life. Not that I didn't before, but now, it's just different. I guess because everything is so much more serious to me. The morning sickness is finally winding down, and I've not picked up too much weight, so no one can really tell. I like having this as me and Khalil's little secret.

On some levels, I'm feeling good because I haven't had too much contact with Shawn. I hate to admit it, but I find myself yearning for him in my weak moments. And, no matter how wrong it is, it is the truth. Not seeing Shawn on a regular basis, or talking to him everyday like we used to, has helped me to move on with my life. The term, "You, me and he," has never been more appropriate. The funny thing is, I love my husband, dearly. I miss my best friend, Shawn, and I may be in love with him, too. What a fucking mess.

We're supposed to meet Shawn and his friend at dinner tonight. It'll be good to see him. I believe I've cried my last tear for him, and Khalil for that matter, so now it's time to focus on me and my baby.

Glancing over to see Khalil's handsome face, he smiles, and places his hand gently across my belly. Resting my ass comfortably in the passenger seat of Khalil's new whip, a black Hummer, I feel like I'm cruising on a Continental flight to Miami. This is a serious load, and Khalil deserves it. He's been working so hard lately, trying to prepare for our new family, getting ready to become a new father and becoming a better father to his daughter. Looking over at him, I return his smile. He's so sweet. He makes me sick one minute, and I love his black ass to death, the next.

"How's my lady, this evening?" Khalil brings my hand to his face and glides it across his cheek, then kissing the palm sweetly.

"I'm good, baby. And excited about dinner."

"Yeah, I haven't let you out in some time. It will be nice to see Shawn. You haven't seen him in like two months, right?"

"Right."

"What's wrong, baby?"

"Nothing, baby. It'll be nice to see Shawn, that's all." I'm trying to maintain my composure, knowing good and damn well, I'm nervous as hell about seeing Shawn again.

"Amber, did I tell you that Shawn has a new girlfriend?"

Saddened, shocked and startled I become when Khalil asks me about Shawn, and his new girlfriend. Of course, I had no idea, and it's not really my place to care, one way or the other. Glancing down at my olive green suede pants, I begin rubbing them with my hand.

"No, I didn't know about Shawn's new girlfriend. That's exciting. I'm so glad he was able to move past Aaliyah." The butterflies in my stomach are floating around, frantically, at an all time high. Why? Who knows? "So, what's her name, Khalil?"

"Summer."

"Summer?"

"Yeah, that's a cool name, right, Amber?"

"Yeah."

"Amber, what's wrong, baby?"

"Nothing, Khalil. Just anxious to go out to eat. I'm hungry."

"Okay, darling. We'll be there in a minute."

Another kiss to my hand.

The soft sounds of Robin Thicke's *Lost Without You* saturate the Hummer gently, and pulls my heartstrings into a million and one directions, as Khalil looks so damn good in his ivory colored, suede coat, with hat to match. The ivory blends so delectably, with his ebony enriched skin. He's so happy to "have me back," as he puts it.

Grinning enchantingly, Khalil looks at me, looking as scrumptious as he possibly can. "You're so beautiful, Amber. And, I'm lost without you."

While the words coming out of Khalil's mouth are endearing and I love him for it, Shawn's face creeps into my psyche and makes me want to cry, all over again, just like I've been doing the last few months.

"I love you, Khalil," I confess, trying to convince him, and me, at the same time.

Thank God, we've arrived at our favorite spot, once again. Delta's, our lovely, soul food restaurant. I heard that tonight is poetry night, and that's right up my alley, along with some candied yams. So, it should turn out to be a lovely evening.

Khalil steps out of the truck, walks around the front, while keeping me in his gaze, and hands the valet—a short, stubby Mexican guy—the keys, opening the door for me, taking my hand, and leading me to the front door of the restaurant. I grab his arm, and hold onto my man tight as we near the entrance. It's packed in here this evening, as the L-shaped bar is filled to capacity.

Khalil leans towards the podium, where the hostess is seated, and tells her that we've got reservations for the evening. Baby girl is about to get slapped, because she's eyeing my man hard as hell, like she's ready to sop him up with a biscuit. Yeah, that's what us black women do; disrespect each other every chance we get. After so much bullshit in recent times, my patience is about as thick and absorbing as a ninety-nine cents store paper towel. I'm simply not having it. So, I give her a I'll-fuck-you-up-quick look and make it clear that we need to be seated.

"Excuse me, Miss. We are *Mr. and Mrs.* Khalil Devereaux, and we have reservations here for six, for eight o'clock. Now, if you can stop staring at my man like a damn fool, and get us seated, I would really appreciate it."

Little brown betty, with her long, awkward looking ass, rolls her neck and looks me up and down, and trust me, I ain't worried, because I look good as shit tonight.

"Sure, Miss. We'll seat you right away."

I know that's right, goddamn it.

The look on Khalil's face is one of astonishment, and utter surprise and I give him a look that lets him know that he can get it real easy too. So, he falls back, just like he's supposed to.

We head to our table, actually, our booth.

Removing my cream-colored shawl, I unwrap it, place it next to me, along with my purse, and slide into my spot. Khalil slides in next to me, and moves my hair off my shoulder, allowing it to flow down my back. He leans in and kisses me on my cheek.

"How are you feeling, Amber?"

"I'm good, Khalil. I feel great, baby." I rub Khalil's hand.

Spotting the waitress approaching, Khalil raises his shoulders at attention. "What are you drinking tonight, Amber? How about a nice, cold glass of milk, sugah?"

A slight giggle escapes me as I respond. "No, Khalil. Just a virgin Piña Colada."

"Are you sure, sweetie?"

"Yes, Khalil."

Finally, our waitress arrives, dressed in all black. "Can I start you off with drinks?"

"Yes, my wife will have a virgin Piña Colada. As for myself, I'll have an Appletini. Oh, and we have four more coming."

"Okay, sir, no problem. I'll bring your drinks right away."

Turning to face Khalil, placing my hand on his thigh, I question him. "Baby, you don't drink Apple Martinis?"

"I know, but I realize it's your favorite drink and you can't have it right now. So I'll drink one for you, baby."

He leans in to give me a tender kiss on my lips. His soft lips taste sweet and forces me to rub my hand up his thigh a bit more. Pulling back from my lips, giving me a look of passion, Khalil tells me, "All right now, Mami. Don't get me started in here." He leans in again, to kiss me once more, when our intimate moment is interrupted.

"Ahem." Keisha clears her throat. And she wasn't lying when she said she was dating Jamal. Look at his ghetto, trifling ass. I know he had something to do with that bachelor party. *Bastard.*

"Yo, what up yo." Jamal gives Khalil a pound.

Unenthusiastically, Keisha says "Hello" to Khalil and slides into the booth next to me.

Jamal speaks, but I barely utter a word, yet remain polite.

"Yo, J. Whatchu drinkin' man? The waitress will be bringing our drinks out in a minute, so be ready."

"Not sure, Khalil. I'll think of something. What you gettin'?"

"I got an Appletini, man."

Bursting out into uncontrollable laughter, Jamal shows us all his pearly yellows, not whites, sitting over there looking like a broke as T.I. "Man, what the fuck? Apple Martini? You bitchin' up on a nigga man?"

Khalil leans back into the tall, leather backing of the chair, bawls up a napkin, and throws it at Jamal's head. "Nah, dumb ass. I'm just chillin' tonight."

"Yeah, okay, K. Sounds like a bitch-ass nigga drink to me."

Keisha, laced in black leather jeans, a white turtleneck top, with a diamond choker, ponytail, and bangs, and high-heeled black, leather boots, interrupts. "Shut the hell up, Jamal. You always gotta sound so fucking stupid every time you go somewhere. You lucky as hell your black ass is light-skinned and convenient, else your ass would be eating some fucking McDonald's tonight. Alone. Don't embarrass me. You know, Greg was right. I'm breaking this shit off, right after you pay for dinner."

We all laugh, well, except for Jamal.

"Yeah, whatever, Keisha."

More laugh out loud humor comes from Keisha and the four of us are bent over in tears. The waitress brings our drinks, takes Keisha's and Jamal's order and asks Khalil if we're ready to order.

"No, Miss, thanks, we're waiting for two more. But bring us some appetizers. An order of buffalo wings, fried cheese, some bread, potato skins, and salad. That should hold us."

"Okay, sir. I will place the order and return once its ready."

"Thank you," I respond, just for two cents purposes.

A delicate pinch to my left thigh, garners my attention and I look at Keisha. Her eyes signal me to look straight ahead, to find Shawn, speaking to one of the poets at the end of the bar, and I can see "Miss Thang" on his side. Damn, Keisha's got some good eyes, because no one else has spotted him. But here he comes, as well as the tidal wave of emotions.

Look at him, sinfully seductive, charming, sweet, and kind, Shawn walks up to the booth, adorning a pearly white, delectable smile and gives Khalil some brotherly love. Dipped in black, he is passion, love, intensity on fire, and I'm praying, right at this moment, that God forgives me, for I know not what I think. Sean John jeans, in dark blue, a mean belt, and heavy black cashmere sweater, which outlines all of his masculinity, forces heads to turn, both men and women.

"Hey, everybody! Long time, no see."

"Yeah, where da fuck you been, nigga?" Jamal sounds just as gutter as he looks.

"I've been around, just working hard lately. Trying to handle business."

"Not to worry, he's in good hands." Girlie tugs on Shawn's arm. "By the way, I'm Summer. Summer Rain Kelly. Nice to meet all of you."

Pointing to each one of us individually, Summer names all of us. "You're Khalil," she points to me, "And you must be Amber. Shawn has said so much about you! Amber this, Amber that!"

Keisha pinches my thigh. I look up, only to find Shawn staring at me. His look is intense, and once again, not like a brother looking at his long, lost sister. I stare back at him. His eyes don't leave mine, as Summer points out Keisha and Jamal and then begins chatting with Khalil. Who the fuck is she, Vanna White? Pointing and revealing every damn thing.

Shawn and Summer take their seats at the booth, as I nervously sip on my colada. The waitress returns and takes all of our orders. We shoot the breeze for a while, enjoying our appetizers and drinks, and the host for the evening, introduces us to poetry night. I'm so excited. The last time I heard some good spoken word, was when Aaliyah and I went together. A memory I wish could erase.

A short, dark-skinned man walks onto the small stage and introduces our first poet. My eyes pass Shawn as they reach the stage, yet Shawn is still staring at me. A slight smirk crosses his luscious lips.

"Greetings, people. We have a special guest tonight. Everyone, give it up for Marc Lacy."

Keisha pinches me more on my thigh, and I can't help but to laugh on the inside because this brother is right up her alley. Tall, light-skinned and well groomed. I prefer the kind of man you can't see at night, myself.

"Peace and Blessings people. I have a special piece to deliver tonight and it comes with a message behind it. Although the person wishes to remain anonymous, he doesn't want his feelings to go unnoticed. He dedicates this to the *only* woman he's ever loved. I call this one, *Point of No Return*."

Looking over towards the poet, my eyes meet and greet Shawn again, and I quickly release my hold on him. All the while, Summer kisses his cheek, feeds him buffalo wings, rubs his hand, wipes his mouth, and kisses his lips. She looks like a woman in love. He smiles from the adoration. *I think I'm going to be sick.*

Khalil gets my attention. "Amber, the poet, Marc Lacy is up now."

*Do you agree
that when a man
loves a woman...
...and a woman
loves a man...
souls, spirits, and bodies
should mesh
to form a collaboration
of predilection
and the partiality
exuded for one another
to one another
is just a measure
of exclusivity?
Do you agree
that when a man
and a woman share
the identical yearn
that both should
feel the warmth
when passion burns?
For today, my heart
possesses an urn
full of potion
comprised of love,
good lust, and
devotion...*

As prone am I
to fall for you
even if 'Mrs. Jones'
is how you answer the phone...

I never considered you
a forbidden lover
for if my heart
forbade such activity,
then your face would not
appear within the limits
of my every fantasy...
Okay, so it's morning,
and you and I never
tallied the costs
beforehand, we just know
that my heart's a love outlet
and you my dear, are its name brand...
See, you are the reason that my libido burns...
I'm in too deep, therefore at the point...OF NO RETURN.
I hope you understand
that in life, whatever feels right
is not necessarily wrong...
For is it who you're with
or could it be where your heart
belongs?
To me, it doesn't matter,
because my reality
is circumscribed within
my head
and I'm never mislead
when it comes to picturing myself

side by side
with a picturesque work of art
who's heart is surrounded by
a bodacious body
crowned with a smiling
epitome of loveliness...
Nonetheless
I desire nothing less
than the best for my
passion's desires...
...and you my friend
are the flame in my fire.
I aspire to
liquefy your loveliness
and drink you
like an essential libation...
That way the intonation
of my heart will
possess the cadence
equivalent to the radiance
of your essence...
I'm a grown man;
but I feel like an
adolescent whose deficit
of adulthood is suppressed
each time you undress...
Blessed do I feel
when I can partake
of the ardent meal
you tend to feed me...
My tenure of slavery
on your plantation

I wish would last forever...
Love is the master
and you've whipped me...
For I pray we'll always be together.
Again, you are the impetus of why my fervor burns...
I'm trapped within your abyss, therefore at the point...OF
NO RETURN.

Shawn's eyes stay glued to my every move as I ask Khalil to please, "excuse me," and I make my way to the ladies room. Locking the stall behind me, I breathe a heavy, panicked breath, and heave over, trying to prevent the tears from flowing.

Keisha enters the bathroom. "Amber!" she yells, approaching my stall. "Bitch, where you at?"

"Yeah, Keisha." I open the stall door and walk towards the sink, patting my face and head with cold water. "Did Khalil say anything?"

"No, Mami. He just said something about you feeling under the weather."

"Okay, good. Let me get back out there. Did you see the way Shawn was staring at me?"

"Bitch, you know I did! Now he done did that shit on the low and I'm sure Khalil noticed nothing. He knows how much Shawn loves you anyway, well, as a little sister. But if he ever finds out the real, you a dead bitch, bitch!" Laughing, Keisha looks deep into my soul, wiping the tear that manages to escape my eye. "Look, Amber. What you two shared was wrong, but I'm really starting to believe there's more to this. Now, take your high-yellow ass back out there to your husband, and do the best you can, bitch. This shit is unreal. Never in my wildest days would I have thought this shit was possible. Shawn loves you something terrible, honey. Shit, look at his ass out there with that pretty bitch, and he drooling over yo' confused ass. Lookin' like he ready to fuck you right now, on the damn stage. He got that poem off though. He's a classy nigga, and he's got you feelin' some kinda way."

Grabbing Keisha's arm for dear life, we head out the bathroom, as Summer walks in.

"Oh, hey, Amber." Summer, looking as gorgeous as someone I would picture Shawn to be with, stands at an attentive five-foot-nine, with a slight bounce to her hips, no stick figure by any means. Curly, long, jet-black hair, with an apple face. Damn, she looks like… me.

"Hi, Summer."

"We'll see you back at the table, Summer," Keisha says as we leave the bathroom.

Arriving back at the booth, Khalil gets up, making room for me to sit, kisses my cheek once more. Summer follows and sits, as Shawn takes a sip of his drink. I glance at him, and I swear he just blew me a kiss.

"Excuse me folks, but I need to make an announcement." Khalil stands to his feet, adorning a picture perfect smile. I can't imagine what he's going to do, but I look on proudly.

"It is with great pleasure that I tell you all, that Amber and I are expecting our first child."

Shawn
Say Yes

A s Summer leans back into the passenger seat of my ride, she cracks the window to allow the cool breeze to sneak in. We decided to head to the restaurant earlier from my loft in the city, since Summer had work in New York today. She parks in front of the loft, which will be really convenient for her when it's time for her to leave. I must admit, I'm enjoying Summer's company, but not ready to settle down with anyone right now. I look over to her, and she stares back at me. It's a look I've seen before, the look of love. I know Summer's falling hard and I can't do anything about that. She is stunning and right up my alley, as far as looks are concerned. And, she's intelligent and has a good head on her shoulders. Could any man ask for more? Yes, she's the perfect woman, but she's not Amber, unfortunately.

I'm not sure, at this moment, if it is the whole forbidden fruit notion that gets in the way of me moving on. Or, if it is true love I feel for her. I know I feel some sort of way about Amber. My stomach knots up when I think of her. It took me weeks to change the sheets after the times I made love to her. Just to inhale her precious scent, provided comfort to my soul. She is the star of my dreams, the want in my need. But, she belongs to my best friend. And now, they're having a baby. There's no way in hell I'll be able to share my life with the true love of my life. But as my momz always told me, "you make your bed, you lie in it." What a predicament. My ex is stalking me, I'm falling for the perfect woman, and the true love of my is married to my best friend.

I remember one of the last times I saw Amber, prior to this evening at dinner. It was about a week after we made love for the first time. Aaliyah was all moved out, and Amber, with her sinfully sweet self, offered to help me clean the loft and to get rid of Aaliyah once and for all. She just called one Saturday morning, and offered to help. That was a day etched into my life's memory. One of those significant occurrences that no matter what life takes you through, or how many years pass, you'll never forget it.

When the doorbell rang, and I headed to the front door to open it, and there, sweet Amber waited. I took Amber by her hand and led her to the couch, kissed her on her cheek along the way. The tension was thick, so thick you could cut through it. I remembered that I was only in boxer briefs, so I excused myself and headed to the den to grab my sweats and tee. I even put my socks on. That's weird, I know. But I felt like I needed to be fully clothed around baby girl. Upon my return, I noticed Amber had removed her sweater, and was now in jeans and a white tee. Simple enough clothing, but for me, a major turn on. I couldn't take my eyes off her breasts and they bounced while she walked from my kitchen back into my living room, holding a glass of orange juice.

"You don't mind, right, Shawn? I haven't had breakfast yet."

Walking toward her, I responded, "No, not at all. I can cook something up real quick for you if you want, Amber. What do you want to eat?"

My eyes followed her lips as she took a sip of her orange juice; I even see the gloss she leaves as an imprint on the rim of the glass.

"I'm not sure. I'll get to cleaning and then I'll decide. I'm cool for now."

After placing her glass onto the kitchen countertop, she walked back into the living room, greeting me with a smile. "I'm ready."

"Okay, cool, baby girl. I got most of it done, but I really needed a woman's touch. Momz is busy down in Virginia and I didn't want to bother her."

"I understand. I'll start upstairs and work my way down. Please give your mother my regards."

"I will. And Amber," I gently grabbed her hand, "Thank you for helping me."

Amber smiled that sweet and endearing smile. That smile that had the ability to melt me from the inside out. We walked upstairs, she headed into the master bathroom, and I began to vacuum my master bedroom.

Several minutes had passed, and not soon after, the smell of Pine-Sol, penetrated my nostrils. A loud crash came from within the bathroom, so I rushed in to see if Amber was all right. Noticing the obvious panic displayed on my face, Amber, as usual, comforted me, in a quiet, soothing voice. "I'm just fine, Shawn. This candle fell from the shelf. I've cleaned it up and will replace the candle, if you tell me where you got it from."

Moving in closer to Amber, I helped her to get up from the bathroom floor. "It's okay. I'll get another one, when I need it." Damn, her hands were so soft I remembered thinking as I caressed them. "Besides, I won't be needing any candles anytime soon, baby girl."

"Why, Shawn?"

"No reason to light them."

Amber stepped out of the bathroom, requested that I put some music on, I guess to create a distraction. I obliged, and put in the first CD I picked up, Floetry.

"The bathroom looks good, Amber, thank you."

"You're welcome, Shawn. I'll finish up in here and then will head downstairs. By the way, you're horrible with this vacuum."
I moved in close to her, after that smart-ass comment, to tease her just a bit. Poking her in her side, then her shoulders, then gave her a tickle to her mid-drift. "Stop Shawn!" She laughed out loud, killing me softly once again with her presence. Moving in closer to her, I played with her some more, grabbed her from behind, and hugged her, and that moment confirmed what I had known all along; Amber was the only one for me. And as the confirmation took hold of me, mind, body and soul, I sang it in her ear, right along with Floetry; "All you gotta do is say Yes."

Turning Amber around, her eyes filled with tears, she pecked me on the lips, and I was ready to make love to her all over again, right there, but my conscience got the best of me. I ignored what I was feeling inside, and just held her tight in my arms, and continued to sing in her ear, "Don't deny what you feel, let me undress you baby."

My trip down memory lane is halted by Summer's sweet voice. "I just wanted to thank you again for a lovely evening." She caresses my hand.

"I'm glad you enjoyed yourself. Khalil and Amber seemed to have a good time too. We'll have to do it again sometime soon."

"I would love that, Shawn."

Although I hear Summer, my mind is somewhere off. I know the whole poetry thing was not cool, but I didn't have a choice.

How else could I get the message across to her? Amber means the world to me. I feel like I'm dying a little more each day I'm not with her. She put it on me something serious.

"So, Shawn, what are you up to this evening?"

Now, Summer is definitely throwing some much-needed distraction into my life. Confusion? Absolutely.

"Nothing much, Summer. I'll probably turn on the NFL channel. See what's up with the Giants. Do you like the Giants, Summer?"

"Not really. I'm not into sports that much."

"Oh, I see. You have to hang around Amber more. She loves the Giants."

"I'd loved to, Shawn."

She smiles that loving, adorable smile to me. If I was in a different stage in my life, Summer could definitely get the business. She could be the one. And I haven't ruled that out, I just need time to sort this out in my heart and mind.

There's some brief silence, so I continue with conversation.

"So, Summer, you got any plans for the weekend?"

"Not really. I mean, I have some work to catch up on, but nothing concrete. Why?"

"Well, if you want to do dinner again, I'm down. I like to watch a lady who enjoys eating."

"Ha, ha! Are you calling me greedy, Shawn?"

I laugh because I knew that was coming. "No, Summer. Not at all. I just like a thick woman, who ain't afraid to eat a cheeseburger, that's all. And you have to admit Summer, that you had fun with those butterfly shrimp earlier this evening."

"So, you don't like thin women? Is that it?"

"Nope, not the least bit. I gotsta have me some ass, Summer. Honestly. I'm not saying that I want a walrus on my arm, but I damn sure don't want a size two either." I laugh out loud and tell her, "Remember sugah, I've been privileged enough to know what's going on under those clothes of yours."

"I see, and you're not complaining. Well, I'm a size twelve. Did you know that?"

"I kind of figured. Amber's a twelve too, I believe."

"Were you two involved, Shawn?"

"What?"

"I'm sorry, didn't mean to pry. It's just that you two were kind of gazing at each other all night. Very weird, sort of like you were newlyweds or something."

Wow, she's thrown me for a loop with that last comment. Was it really like that? I don't think so. Naw, no way. I'm ready to switch gears with the conversation now.

"No, Summer. Amber's like my little sister. We've been cool for over a decade now. Nothing like that. Never. Khalil's my boy, like my brother. We're all family, sweetie."

I can't believe I just lied to her. Back in the day, I'd be preaching to Khalil about how he shouldn't string women along, how he has to step it up, or how he should become a man. It hurt like a muthafucka when the shoe is on the other foot. Pussy, and good pussy at that, can fuck your life up.

"Okay, Shawn. You're such a sweet man. I could really have some fun with you."

Oh, shit now. I knew she was trying to get the business. "Is that right? I thought we had some fun the other night."

"Yes, that's absolutely right, Shawn. Whenever you want some fun, holla at me. We did have fun, but there's more in store, if you'll allow it. There's no need for you to be alone tonight. Matter of fact, you shouldn't be going to bed alone on any night." Summer moves in close, giving me a soft kiss on my lips. "Do you hear me, Shawn?" She moves in more, placing her hand onto my crotch, kissing me once again on my lips. I'm going to crash this ride if she keeps this shit up.

"Yes, I hear you, Summer." I lick her cherry flavored lip-gloss off of my lips, regaining my composure and continue with my drive into the city.

Turning on my Sirius satellite radio, sets the mood for the remainder of the ride over to my loft. Summer, now with my free hand, in hers, takes each of my fingers and sucks on them slowly. The soft kisses from her wet mouth, feels damn good, and she's going to get it with a quickness if she doesn't cut this shit out. While preparing to say something sexy to her, Amber floods my mind, and an eerie feeling takes over me, as something just doesn't feel right. That, and the fact that my cell phone rings. My Bluetooth is in place, so I answer.

"Hello?"

"Shawn, is that you?"

"Yes, it's me. Who else did you think would answer the phone?"

"Can I come to see you?"

"I told you before, and I will tell you again, no. And, I'm busy right now. Bye."

"Wait, Shawn. Please, I have something to tell you, it's important."

"What is it? Tell me now."

"I need to tell you in person, Shawn."

Summer is looking at me as if I have two heads. But I want to continue this conversation. This serves as an incredibly awkward moment.

"You're not pregnant, are you, Aaliyah?"

Summer's eyes are wide and bright, as if she just snorted some cocaine.

"No, Shawn, I'm not."

"Well then, we have nothing to talk about. Bye."

I look at Summer, and apologize for the phone call. "Look Summer, I told you about my ex, and that was her. I apologize if I've disrespected you."

"No problem, honey, her loss, my gain." She smiles and returns to my fingers, I guess as a sign of what's to come.

We pull behind Summer's ride, right in front of my loft. Summer seems anxious to get into my crib, and she's sort of pushing me into the house. Placing the key into the keyhole, I turn the doorknob. In the meantime, Summer's grabbing my ass, pressing her breasts against my back, and I feel my nature rise. I step into the foyer and turn the alarm off. Something strange about this evening. Can't quite put my finger on it, but I feel weird. Summer drops her bag, grabs my face, and begins to kiss me passionately, tongue swirling and dancing a jig in my mouth. Unbuttoning my shirt, hurriedly, she's breathing so heavy, and exhaling deeply to my every touch. I've only grabbed her waist, and she's ready to pop. My hands roam to her round, plump ass and I hold on for dear life.

"Damn, Shawn. I want you to fuck me right here, right now, please," Summer whispers, as she removes her blouse, exposing a pink lace under wire bra that's sexy as hell. She's got the dick long, so yeah, I'm ready, but I'm also feeling like I need to slow this down a bit.

"Summer, don't you think we should slow this down a little."

"Why, Shawn?" She bites and licks my neck.

I lean in to close and lock the front door. "I don't want to move too fast, Summer."

"We're not, baby. I just need to have you right now, Shawn, that's all."

Unbuttoning my pants, she unloosens my belt, reaches in to my crotch and feels the thick swelling between my thighs.

"Mmmm, that's just what I love. This big, hard dick. Damn, Shawn, you're going to make me loose my mind."

Kissing her back passionately, I match every one of her tongue maneuvers, and then proceed to bite and lick her neck. Moving down to her bra, I tug at it with my teeth. She reaches to pull her breast out for me, when my cell rings again. I haven't turned off the Bluetooth, so I decide to answer, get rid of Aaliyah's crazy ass, and then get me some ass.

Summer's still kissing me softly, as I answer the phone. "Hello?"

"Yo, Shawn, man, Amber is trippin'. Has she called you?"

I push away from Summer. "No, man. Haven't heard from her. What happened?"

"She's just mad at me for making the announcement at dinner."

"About the baby?"

"Yeah, man."

"You know how women are when they're pregnant, K. She'll calm down. She probably went over to Keisha's or Scott's."

"You're probably right."

"Why was she so mad?"

"She said she wanted to be the one to tell you, man. She's buggin'."

"Well, I'll reach out to her, K. I'll finish up with Summer and head over there."

"Thanks, man."

"No doubt."

Summer's look of disappoint is evident and I feel so bad at this moment.

"Summer, I will make it up to you. I have to get over to Khalil's."

"What's wrong with Amber, Shawn?"

"I don't know, she's going through some hormonal changes, most likely." I peck her on the lips. "Listen, sweetie, we'll have some time together soon. Call me when you get home so I know you made it safe."

I hand Summer her handbag, and open the door for her.

"Okay, Shawn, let me know if you need me."

After Summer leaves, I pace throughout the first floor of my loft. Why would Amber be so mad at Khalil for that? I don't feel right. This is one of those weird, Twilight Zone days, and I can't put my finger on it. What the fuck is going on?

Reaching for my car keys, I button up my shirt and pants, and dial Amber's cell phone. The phone rings on my end, but seems like it's ringing in real time, like real life. As the phone rings on my end, now on number two, I can hear the phone ringing elsewhere. I open the front door, and the source of the ringing is revealed. Amber, angelic and sweet, is standing at my front door. It's going to be a long night.

Amber
What's Done In The Dark

Why am I here at Shawn's loft, again? Seems as though, I have some serious soul searching in store for my immediate future. Whatever the case, I need to address what my internal issues are. Only one of the two men I'm in love with even know that I am, indeed, in love with two men. This will never work. And how can I make it work? There's no way, no use. As horrible as it sounds, I love my husband with all my heart and soul. And, I love his best friend. I miss Shawn so much, and didn't realize how much until I saw him earlier this evening at dinner.

Shawn opens the door, and I feel like a fucking fool for standing here. He smiles, but then his smile is quickly replaced by a look of curiosity, and I don't blame him, not at all. I'm curious too, as to why I'm really here. I return his smile, and step into his loft, otherwise known as "the secret garden." How did I get into this mess? My heart races. I feel a lump in my throat. I'm so excited, nervous, elated, confused and it's only been five seconds.

Walking into the loft, I take my coat off, and toss it on the sofa. "Did I disturb an important phone call?"

"No, Amber. Not at all. I was just speaking with Summer."

"Is that right?"

"Yes."

"Hmmm."

"Hmmm, what, Amber? She just left, and on her way home. She had a nice time with us."

"I see."

"You see what, Amber?"

Moving in close as hell to Shawn, I stare him deep in the eyes because I need the truth from him.

"Are you two serious, Shawn?"

"Why, Amber?"

"Just curious."

"Wait a minute. Amber. What are you doing here?"

"I wanted to talk to you. It's been a minute."

"So, aren't you supposed to be at home? You could've called."

"Yes."

"So, why are you here, Amber? Are you okay?"

"I'm fine, Shawn. I'm a little mad at Khalil and decided to head over here instead of arguing with him. You know I don't like to argue."

"Well, as long as everything is okay. That's all that matters."

"Well, Shawn, as a matter of fact, everything is not okay."

"What's wrong, Amber?"

I take Shawn's hand and brush it against my face, and then I kiss his inner palm. I have no idea why, either. He smells so good, just like I remember. The sweet smell of Joop mixed with his skin is both a combination of divinity and purgatory for me.

"Amber, no, please. I can't, baby."

"Shawn, please. I need you so bad."

"Amber, baby, we just can't do this."

"You love her don't you?"

"Who?"

"Summer!"

"Is that what this is about? Me and another woman?"

"No, Shawn, it's not. But I can't watch you love someone else."

"Amber. Listen. You have no right to come in here and tell me who I can and can't love. I'm in love with you and you already let me know that I can't love you. Now, you wanna step in my home and tell me that I can't love someone else?"

Placing my arms around Shawn's neck, I pull him into me, kissing him like my life depends on it. Like he somehow, in some weird way, belongs to me, and in my darkest hour, I wish he did.

"Shawn, I love you. Ain't nothing changed about that."

"Amber, go home."

"No!"

"What do you want from me, Amber? You won't let me love you! You refuse to be mine! What the fuck do you want from me?"

"I want you, Shawn!" I scream. "I love you, Shawn! Damn it! I love you! I've always loved you, Shawn! Can't you see that? Do you understand that? Dumb ass! I'm in love with you!"

"You don't want me, Amber! You want Khalil. Go and be his wife. I can't do this anymore."

I back up from Shawn's massive hold of me. Looking him deep in the eyes, I expel, "So, that poem wasn't for me?"

Shawn moves further away from me. Looks at me almost as if he's scared. I still question why I'm truly here.

"Amber, I love you, but you're torturing me. I can't do this anymore. Not to you, not to me, not to…."

Khalil. Oh God, what am I doing? We both know this is so wrong. I love Shawn and I love Khalil. Shawn, whose always been the voice of reason, snaps into a sense of both rationality, consciousness and reality.

"Amber, you're the only woman for me, but I can't do this to you or Khalil, or…"

"Or what, Shawn?"

"Or, the baby, Amber." Shawn looks at me as if I just slit his throat. He moves in close to me, kisses my forehead, and holds me dearly, tenderly, and sweetly. "Is that my child, Amber? Is that why you're here? This all makes sense now. Khalil said you were mad that you didn't have the opportunity to tell me. Now, you're here, screaming at the top of your lungs about me being in love with another woman. Something's up, Amber. I need to know. Is that my child you're carrying?"

"Shawn, I love you so much. I just don't know what to do."

"Well, if you truly love me, Amber, then you need to be with me. I'm yours for the taking."

"But, I love Khalil, too."

"I know you do. But your heart is with me, Amber, and you know it. You need to tell me if you want to be with me, because I know you do."

Shawn leans in and kisses me softly. I melt inside. I miss his touch, embrace, and how me made me feel so loved and comforted. I miss being adored by him.

"Make love to me, Amber. I don't care anymore. If I can't have you, I'll have the memory of your touch and caress. I'll settle for anything at this point. It's hard to breathe without you, baby girl. You messed me up real bad."

"I'm scared, Shawn."

"Me too, Amber."

The touch of Shawn's fingertips stroking my arms and his massive, yet gentle, hands rubbing my shoulders, sends all types of emotions through my entire being. This is so wrong, but Shawn is in my system.

"There's only one woman for me, Amber." Shawn kisses my shoulder, as he removes my blouse. "And like I said, you've got me past the point of no return." As his mouth moves from my shoulder to my lips, I smell his scent, along with the glimpse of hope in his eyes as he leans in to kiss my lips, then my forehead. I'm so very anxious, and nervous and guilty, all at the same time. If loving him is wrong, I guess, I really don't want to be right.

"I love you so much, Amber. My heart aches when I'm not with you. You invade all my fantasies. You're the star of all my wet dreams. I pray for your happiness and your safety each morning that I rise. You mean the world to me." Shawn lifts me and carries me up the same flight of stairs, in which this love triangle originated. I kiss his lips as the tears fall from my eyes.

As we move closer to the place where our hearts will be able to soar free, Shawn looks at me, deeply into my eyes. "Summer."

"What?"

He puts me down, and backs down a few stairs. "Amber, I'm just as torn as you. I love you so much, but I can't do this to Summer. She's been too good to me."

Panic sets in as I try to take in Shawn's rejection. Grabbing my hand, he leads me back down the stairs.

"No more lies, Amber. There's been too much betrayal going on. Summer may be the one for me, but because of my love for you, I haven't given her all of me. She deserves better, Amber. And so does Khalil."

"But, what about us, Shawn?"

"Us happened because we were both vulnerable and betrayed, and we were able to comfort each other. Amber, I will always be in love with you, and I wish you were mine."

"I want to be yours, Shawn," I reveal, pulling him closer to me.

"Don't make this harder than it already is, Amber."

The doorbell interrupts our moment of indecision.

Khalil
Déjà vu

D riving on the New Jersey Turnpike on a clear winter night should be a lovely experience, as it has been for so many years for Amber and me. Tonight, however, is definitely not a lovely night. I can't believe this shit. Why is my baby acting so weird? I tell everyone about one of the happiest things going on in our lives, and she starts trippin'. It could be the stress of finding the bruises on Lex, her hormones have kicked into overdrive, or maybe she really wanted to be the one to tell everyone, especially Shawn. But it just doesn't make much sense.

Honestly, Amber hasn't been one hundred percent since she discovered my fuck up. She has become so patient and forgiving over the years, I think that time broke the camel's back, for real. Funny thing is, and it is probably of no consolation, but I've never cheated on my *wife*. Yes, my *wife*. Since Amber and I have been married, I've been dedicated to her as a devoted husband. I've sewn my oats, I've played the field, I've been there and done that, and have made every effort to refocus my very existence on Amber, and building my family. But really, how much can one person take?

When I think back on all of the times I've done my woman wrong, I can't really blame Amber for anything. Although, I don't see how my telling our friends of her pregnancy would justify her leaving the house to "get some air." Looking in the mirror is no joke. Most people don't do it because it forces them to discover who they really are. So much easier to point the finger at this or that, to place blame where it's not supposed to be. I've reevaluated who I am. And, the person I used to be, I don't like too much. Amber stayed with me. I don't deserve her.

My heart is pounding so very hard, and my nerves are shot, as I take this voyage to confirm my suspicions. Is Amber really loving my best friend? How did I come to this? At dinner tonight, she was just some sort of way, especially when she saw Shawn. I know she hasn't seen Shawn in quite some time, but, well I don't know. She's always run to Shawn whenever we had our problems, and my boy was always there, and Amber always forgave me. But, could Shawn and Amber have–? Naw, I'm buggin' right now. I'm so fucked up right now because of my baby girl, Lex. I choke up every time I think about her abuse. She's with momz now so I can calm Amber down. Besides, she loves playing with Candy and Chandy, and momz loves her some Lex. She thinks Lex looks just like her.

Just to think, the same tramp I was running around with is the same slut who is beating my daughter's ass. Karma is a muthafucka, and the sins of the father trickle down to the child. I gotta make this right for my baby, but I can't do it without Amber. I need her in my life and can't imagine my life without her presence there constantly. I remember when Amber found out about me and Shayla. I was stupid enough to succumb to Shayla's advances right in my dorm room.

I was off for the day, had no classes on Wednesday. That's how I set up my schedule because I wanted a chill day for me.

Even back then, I had dreams of owning my own business and becoming an entrepreneur, so Wednesdays was my day to do research and fact finding for my business. From self help books, to oral presentations, I studied everything. Only because of Amber. She would come on Wednesday afternoons, to help me write a proposal or listen to a speech, or help me to construct a business plan. She was my rock then, just like she is my rock now. But, that one day, one out of two, I'll always regret, was the day she caught me with Shayla.

"*Yo, Khalil. When you gonna leave your girl, and chill with me?*"

"*Shayla, I told you, I'm not leaving Amber. But I still wanna have fun with you.*"

We listened to Guy's Let's Chill, *as we laid on my twin-sized bed, in my dorm room. Shayla had this short haircut, that framed her pretty face so well. She was the bomb; a bad girl, indeed, and turned me on in the worst way. She was digging me hard, and I was digging that ass harder. She would let me fuck her in her ass anytime I wanted, and boy she could suck a dick like she was sucking a golf ball through a garden hose. Really nasty and slut like, and it fucked me up. But she was falling in love.*

"*K, I'm really falling for you. We've been having so much fun, but I want more. I need more from you, K. Don't you like what we have?*"

"*I do Shayla.*" *I kissed her softly on her pouty lips.* "*You mean a lot to me.*"

"*Well then, be with me.*" *After she made that comment, my jimmy was on swole, not due to the comment itself, but just the way she looked at me, like I was the only person that mattered in her life; like I was her reason for existence. She worshipped the ground I walked on. She glanced down and saw the rise of my* nature. *"See, K. We meant to be together, Boo," she told me as she tongue kissed me real deep and allowed her hands to roam freely to my crotch. "Let me suck your dick, K."*

"Shayla, Amber will be here any minute. Not today."

"Well, baby, slide in my ass real quick, I promise not to make a sound."

I couldn't resist. I knew Shawn wouldn't be back for hours, as his Wednesdays were full with classes, and then he'd end up in campus ministry to pray. Amber wouldn't be by for at least another hour or two.

Shayla stripped, but left those high-heeled open-toed sandals on, which turned me on like crazy. I mounted her on the bed, and dropped my sweats. She had already greased my dick with Vaseline. My shit was like a steel pole. I slid the tip in and then inched the rest of my manhood into her. Shayla had the prettiest ass and I thought I was in heaven. Sliding in and out of her, had me in a state of uninhibited lust, as I closed my eyes, and rocked her hard and slow. The fact that we had to be quiet provided more of a turn on.

A loud crash of glass breaking interrupted my dirty deed, and I looked over to see Amber standing there, mouth agape, and tears streaming down her cheeks. She had picked up lunch and two Snapples for us, and dropped one on the floor. She turned around and ran down the hall. I pulled out of Shayla's ass, pulled up my sweats and ran after her, while Shayla laughed her ass off.

God protects babies and fools. Right? Well, He protected me by giving my foolish ass another, well, many other chances with Amber. What a fool am I. But, what about my baby, Lex? Has He protected her? I know I'm stressing, questioning God.

As I pull up in front of Shawn's loft, the butterflies in my stomach want to fly off into some far away place, where it's nice and safe, and the hurt and pain of love and life doesn't exist. A say a silent prayer as I walk up the stairs, and hope that I don't find Amber and my best friend compromised, the same way Amber found me and Shayla, and Cookie, and Peaches, and so many countless others. The prospect of tasting my own medicine is dreadful. I reach the top of the stairs and ring the doorbell.

"I never thought you would be that dirty nigga, Shawn," I accuse as he opens the door to his loft.

Shawn looks at me like I'm crazy, and Amber, side by side with my best friend, screams, "Khalil!"

As I pull out my thirty-eight revolver from my inside jacket pocket, tears stream down my face, and pour relentlessly from my eyes. Pointing the tip of the barrel next to Shawn's temple, I tell him to come outside. "Get the fuck out of the house, Shawn, so I can blow your muthafuckin' head off, bitch."

As Shawn raises his hands, like he's being interrogated by one of New York's finest, he steps out of the loft, and Amber follows, still screaming, "Khalil! What's wrong with you?"

Pressing the tip closer to Shawn's temple, I lean in to my boy. "You really had me fooled for a while." With a heavy, panicked laugh, I sigh. "You're in love with my wife! I can't believe this shit is happening."

"Listen, K." Shawn tries to lower his arms.

Taking my free hand, I cold cop the shit out of Shawn, punching him hard has hell in his face, and his head cocks to the side. I motion with that same hand for Amber to come to me.

"Get your ass over here, Amber!" I motion with my finger to the space beside me. Amber stands still and doesn't budge. I've frightened her.

"Yo, K, what the fuck? Nothing happened, Khalil, man, I'm telling you!" Shawn backs up from the tip of my barrel. I should kill this bitch right now.

"Look, Shawn." More tears flow down my cheeks. "I don't care what happened, and I don't want to know what happened, all I know is now, right now, I'm taking my wife home, and I don't ever want to see you again, never in my life."

Shawn lowers his head, and Amber goes over to him, hugs him, and consoles him. Shawn returns my gaze, looking straight at me, with tears profusely pushing their way out of his eyes. "Khalil, nothing happened."

"Khalil! Put the gun down!" Yelling, Amber reaches for the gun.

"I can't believe this shit here. Well, yes, I can." Aaliyah walks up the stairs to Shawn's loft. "All of this time, I'm crying over you, and begging you to take me back. All this time, you've been in love with Amber, Shawn?"

Shawn looks at Aaliyah in disgust. I lower the gun and now it hangs near my thigh. "Aaliyah, I told you it's over and I don't know why you came here tonight."

"Yes, you know why the fuck she came here tonight, you dumb nigga," Shayla yells to Shawn as she appears out of nowhere, at Aaliyah's side, walking up the stairs along with her. "So, K, did you know yo' boy fuckin' yo' precious wife? See, you so fuckin' smart, K!"

"Shut the fuck up, Shayla!" I yell at her. "Why are you here anyway?"

Moving up another step, Shayla steps to Amber, all in her face, real close like she wants to fuck her up something awful. Speaking to me, she looks Amber dead in her face. "K, you shoulda stayed with me. We had a good life together, K. Now look at you," Shayla tells me while staring at Amber.

Amber moves closer in to Shayla's face. "He has a good life, Shayla."

Amber's cell phone rings, loud as shit, and she decides to pick it up. Talk about timing.

"Yeah, I'm okay. At Shawn's house. Shayla's here. Aaliyah's here. Khalil's here. Now here comes Summer," she says to the person on the other end of the phone.

We all look at the bottom of the stairs and see that Summer is approaching. "Shawn, are you okay? I left something here so I turned around." Summer looks up at me and sees the gun. "Khalil, why do you have a gun?"

"It's nothing, baby, everything is okay," Shawn tells Summer.

With a laugh only the devil could create, Shayla looks Summer up and down. "Oh hell naw, everything ain't okay. Why you lyin' to "baby," Shawn?"

Summer looks at Shayla. "Who are you?"

"Oh, you ain't heard about me. Bitch, don't worry 'bout who I am. What you need to fuckin' deal wit is yo' man, fuckin' his best friend's wife."

"Shawn," Aaliyah yells and points to Summer. "Shawn, who is this woman?"

Shawn tries to make it down the stairs to see Summer, but I'm still not convinced of shit, so his ass ain't going anywhere. Again, I place the tip of my gun to Shawn's temple. "Ain't nobody going nowhere until I figure this shit out."

"Shawn," Summer yells. "Baby, is this true? Are you sleeping with Amber?"

"No, Summer, I'm not. Amber just came over to talk. We're not sleeping together, Boo."

"Okay, Shawn. I believe you. Come to my house so we can talk please." Summer reaches out for his hand.

Aaliyah steps in to split the two of them apart. With tears running down her face, Aaliyah gets into Summer's face. "Shawn, I can't believe you said you love this woman!"

"Well, I do love her!" Shawn yells then looks at me. "Khalil, man. Put the gun down. I know you're stressed right now."

Amber jumps in. "Khalil, please baby. Let's go home."

She then hunches over, grabs her belly. "Oh, no, not the baby!"

I rush over to my wife, and hold her for dear life. "Amber, are you okay?"

"Khalil, please stop. I can't take this stress, please Khalil, give me the gun."

Panic sets into my soul when I realize what's taken place. I actually put a gun to my boy's head and accused him of fucking my wife. Okay, maybe the Lexis news and all has me stressed too. Shawn looks at me, as I put the gun away, back into my inside jacket pocket.

The sound of a siren interrupts all of the chaos and the police are in a squad car, in the middle of the street. The heavy set white officer, rolls down his window, looks up at all of us. "Is everything okay up there? We got a report about a gun."

Shawn walks down the stairs, and Summer follows. Summer pulls out her government badge, showing her license and gun to the officer. "We're just fine, officer." Shawn points to Summer, while she hands the officer her credentials. "This here is Summer Kelly, she works for immigration. She's my girlfriend. We're all old college buddies just reuniting for the evening, that's all."

Summer steps in.

"Yes, officer, just catching up on old times."

The cop looks Summer up and down, and tells Shawn, "You got a good one, she's a keeper."

Shawn puts his arm around Summer's neck. "Yes, I know, officer. Sometimes you have to go through hell to find heaven."

Summer smiles and kisses Shawn on the lips.

"Well, seems like all is well. I'll call it in as a false alarm," the officer tells Shawn.

"Thanks man."

As Shawn and Summer walk back to the porch, a car flies up to the front of the loft, at maximum speed. Blasting the sweet sounds of Jill Scott's *Whatever* is Scott. Scott, dressed in all black from head to toe, gets out of the car, and comes to the porch. This is déjà vu all over again.   Rushing up the flight of stairs, he stops mid way and looks Aaliyah up and down. "Haven't you gone off and tried to kill yourself yet? I mean do you really have anything else to live for?" Scott says to Aaliyah, as he walks by her and up the stairs toward Amber, but turns around to see Summer. "Summer? What are you doing here?"

"Scott, I'm with Shawn. We've been together for some time now."

"Is that right? You never told me, Summer."

Amber jumps in to the conversation. "Scott, what are you doing here? And how do you know Summer?"

"Baby girl, I'm here because I knew some shit was going down. And I am fully prepared to fuck up as many niggas as I have to tonight. And, I been knowin' Summer. Her brother Shane and I are kickin' it. And honey, he is all that and a bag of chips, and a bottle of Cristal. But that's for another day."

Shayla walks up to Scott. "Who tha fuck you think you talkin' to, faggot ass nigga?"

Scott turns around and looks at all of us with a raised brow. He starts wailing his arms in mid air, stomps his feet and starts jumping up and down. He looks and Amber and smiles. "Amber, please tell me this bitch ain't Shayla! Please tell me, Amber.

'Cause if this skank-cunt-ho is Shayla, yo' huzbin' baby mama, oh see, I'ma fuck her ass up real quick."

"Yeah, nigga, I'm Shayla. You got somethin' ta say, say it to me, you fag."

Scott gets all up in Shayla's face, points his finger right between her eyes. He turns his head around, facing me. Finger still in Shayla's face, he says, "See, Khalil. I hope your black ass has learned a lesson. You lie with dogs, well, stankin' ass bitches in this case, and you end up with fleas." He turns back around to Shayla. SLAP! He smacks the hell out of her. "And bitch, call me a fag one mo' again, and I'll have you and yo' foul ass ditsy sister sucking *my* dick."

"Scott!" Summer yells. "They're not worth it!"

"Summer's right, Scott. They're not worth it. What Shayla needs to do is worry about her child. Who she has been abusing," Amber tells Scott and gets into Shayla's face. "Because if I have my way, Shayla, you won't be seeing your daughter anymore. You's a sorry ass bitch."

Shayla looks up at me. "K, where's Lex?"

"Don't worry about it, Shayla. She's fine, better than she's been with you."

"Nigga, where's my daughter?"

"Shayla, I told you she's fine. How did you get here anyway?"

"Nigga, I went by yo' house and you wasn't there, so Aaliyah dumb ass wanted to come over here to beg Shawn bitch ass to take her back. I came up here to get my daughter."

I walk down the stairs to move close into her face, invading her space. With jaws tight and teeth clenched, I make my point undoubtedly clear. "My daughter will be with me, *always*. You won't get a chance to beat on her *ever* again."

Shayla gets all up in my face, kisses my lips and I back off. She pulls me in closer, bites the bottom of my lips and pushes me in my chest, sending me back a few steps. "Well, guess what, K? She *ain't* yours. *She ain't yours.*"

Six months later...

Shawn
Genesis

Happy Mother's Day!" I yell to my mother as she opens the door to the town home I purchased for her about a year ago. I told her to come up to the city with me, but she refused. Her friends are here, family members too. This is home for her. I respect that. I offered to buy her a single-family home, equipped with new appliances, sunroom, master bedroom and all, but she just wanted something small and quaint. Didn't want me spending too much money on her, she said. I told her money was no issue, not that I am Rockefeller or anything near it, but my momz deserves the best. I tell her that all the time.

Her smile could light up my darkest hour, and always makes me feel warm and lifted inside. Standing at a petite five-foot-five, my mother wears her small frame well. Her chocolate brown skin is just like mine. I even have her full lips. My large stature comes from my father. The bastard. Thank the good Lord my common sense was handed to me directly from momz. She instilled in me a strong work ethic, amongst other things. I love her to death, which is why I left the city behind, and Summer too, to be with my mom this weekend. I wanted this Mother's Day to be special for her. Plus, I needed the break, a little getaway from the fast pace. I have some good news to share with momz, and honestly need to get her opinions on a few things so that I can continue moving forward with my life.

Reaching down, I peck my mom on the cheek and give her a soft kiss. Revealing the oversized flower bouquet from behind my back, I hand them to her. Her radiant smile melts my insides.

"Oh, Shawn! These are beautiful baby." Momz backs up, and opens the door to her town home wide. "Come on in, baby."

"Thank you, Mom."

I wipe my feet on the mat at the front door. A hunter green door mat, with the words Jesus is Lord written in bold white. I make sure I clean the bottom of my feet before entering, because momz can and will go upside my head if I dare walk into her home, the one I purchased, with dirty shoes. She's the reason why I am so neat and clean. I keep my home meticulous, and I owe that to her. Summer always compliments me on how well my house is organized and structured. Well, Summer compliments me on just about everything. Something about that girl. I want and need for absolutely nothing since I've been with her.

Walking further into the town home, I smile and let out the biggest sigh and then a huge laugh as I see the pictures of me and my mom. She has them on the fireplace mantle, and on top of the piano. A brass plant holder, with glass shelving was meant to hold her plants and flower arrangements, but she's managed to make that a portrait studio. Walking over to the brass stand, I see a picture of me. I had to be about eight months old in this photo right here. I hold it up and see that she's had it restored. A chic gold frame holds it dear. I'm compelled to ask her why in the name of Jesus she would display such a picture. I put my overnight bag down on the floor and rub the front of the picture. Turning around to yell for my mom, I see she's already standing there with tears in her eyes.

"Mom, why are you crying?"

"I'm crying, because I'm so proud of you, Shawn." She walks over to hug me and I wrap my hand around her waist, giving her a peck on her forehead.

"Mom, I am who I am, because of you."

"Oh, Shawn."

A huge grin dances across my face. "But, mom..."

"Yes, baby?"

"Why do you have a picture of me butt naked in the living room for everyone to see?"

She snatches the picture from me and laughs. "Because you look so cute in the bathtub. This is one of my favorite pictures of you. Now put my picture back, it's my property, and yes, Shawn, it's staying right there." Reaching up, she places the picture back in its original spot. "Now, come on, baby. Mama made you dinner."

"Mom!"

"What, baby?"

"It's Mother's Day weekend, mom. We're supposed to be going out to dinner. Hello?"

A punch lands on my arm, I guess, in response to my "hello" comment.

"Now listen here, son. You may tower over me, but don't forget mama can still beat your ass."

"Mom!"

Momz places her hand on her hips and pouts. "Well, I can. And don't think I won't."

I laugh out loud. She's got to be the coolest mother on the planet. "I know, mom. I'm shivering all over."

"You better be. Now, we can go out to dinner tomorrow. You're staying the weekend, right?"

"Yes, mom."

"Okay, well bring your big self in this here kitchen and let me feed my baby, please."

"Okay, mom."

"Sugar, I fixed up the guest bedroom for you. Fresh linens on the bed, and there's a television in there with cable and everything. I want you to be comfortable. Go put your things in there, and I'll make your plate."

As I walk through Momz's town home, I smile more. She has it hooked up in here really sweet. The burgundy plush sofa set is complimented by ivory carpet. The mahogany piano in the living room gives the huge room an elite touch. A brick, floor-to-ceiling fireplace has wood in it. I guess for show, because it is May. I hope momz isn't losing it. On either side of the fireplace is African American art that I bought for her. The paintings are a matching set, with mahogany, cherry frame. A roadway, with a cross at the end, and a black woman standing at the beginning of the roadway. When I saw these paintings, I immediately had to buy them because the woman reminded me of my mother. On the road to glory, and yes, with many miles to travel. Her road has been intensely rough, which is why she'll never have to work another day in her life, if I have anything to do with it.

"Mom, the place looks good," I yell to her as I walk up the stairs to reach the bedroom.

"Well, I ain't got nothing to do, Shawn. You won't let me work. All I do is fix up the house and work on my garden. I made some of my collard greens."

After placing my bags onto the bed in the guestroom, I notice my college graduation photo on the nightstand. It's a photo of Amber, Khalil and me all in our caps and gowns. Amber's in the middle, Khalil is to the left and I am to the right. I pick up the picture and smile and reminisce about the good old days. I remember when Khalil and I shared a dorm room in school. One day, he came back to the room, and ranted and raved about this new girl he met.

I was busy listening to my EPMD tape, and getting my study on. Khalil busted in the room yelling.

"Yo, Shawn, man, I'm telling you. This redbone honey, I think her name is Amber, man. Damn! Yo, she a big girl too. Big ass titties man. You know I love that shit!"

Looking puzzled, I looked up at him.

"Who?"

With a high top fade, and a Karl Kani tracksuit, Khalil sits next to me on my bed. "Yo, Shawn. I'm telling you, man. I met this fine redbone honey. She fine, Shawn. And I think she a virgin. Damn, she look so sweet. And she thick. Man, I'm telling you. I'm gonna pop that cherry real nice."

"What she look like?"

"Shawn, are you listening?"

"Man, you talking so fast. Slow down."

"Okay, Shawn. Man, her name is Amber. Amber Clarke. I talked to her in the cafeteria today. I been eyeing her for a minute. Man, she got that curly hair. Pretty full lips. Shawn, she got some big ass titties, man. Thick thighs. I'm telling you, Shawn. I'm gonna beat that pussy up, for real."

"Is that right?"

"Word up, man. Like Eric B. and Rakim say it, 'I'm gonna get Paid in Full, bro.'"

"Wait a minute, K."

"What Shawn?"

"Does she carry a pink Adidas book bag?"

"Uh, yeah I think so. I think she likes pink. She had on this pink top today man. Titties was like, Poooowwwwww! Look at me, I'm here!"

"She got gray eyes, K?"

"Yeah man! Damn, man. I'm telling you, Shawn. Yeah, she got them pretty ass cat eyes too. I'm gonna look her straight in her eyes when I'm tapping that high yellow ass."

"Are you serious, K?"

"Yeah, brother, what's up with you, Shawn?"

"That's the girl I was telling you about, K. Amber. Amber Clarke. I told you we became friends because we're in the same English class. I told you, man, that I was going to ask her out. I told you last week that I met this girl that I was really digging and that I wanted to ask her out, man."

"Yeah, Shawn?"

"Yes, Khalil."

"Oh, sorry man. I'll back off."

"Naw, K, you already asked her out. She had no clue I was even interested."

"You sure, man?"

"Yeah, I'm sure."

I remember that day from time to time and always wonder, what if? What if I had stood tall, firm in my convictions and told my boy that I wanted to get with Amber? Would I be married to her right now? Would I have taken her through such turmoil? Khalil probably would have gone off and fucked the next girl, her friend, the sister, aunt, and moved on to the next set of bitches with a heartbeat. Thankfully, my man has grown and I believe he's finally got it. Got the message that when you have a good woman, don't fuck it up. Women always say a good man is hard to find. Shit, a good woman is harder to find. Nowadays, bitches want a man with bling, money, cars and fancy things. It's hard to find a real woman who is interested in real things.

Amber is in good hands now, as Khalil has stepped up to the plate and is handling business. But, a part of me will always wonder. I think of her often, more often than I should, but it's all in perspective now. She is someone that I will always be in love with and have undying affection for. But it wasn't meant to be and I refuse to block my blessings. Because of my fiasco with Aaliyah and my confusion over Amber, God opened my eyes, heart and mind, and sent Summer my way. And I ain't fucking that shit up.

"Ahem." Momz clears her throat as she stands at the door. "Reminiscing huh?"

"Yes, mom. I can't believe you still have this picture."

"My baby graduated college that day, sweetie. I'll have that picture, always."

"Mom?" I turn around to look at her as I put the picture back down onto the nightstand.

"Yes, baby."

"I'm so happy in my life right now, but I am also confused. Well, maybe not confused, but torn. Oh, forget it, it's nothing."

Mom walks into the bedroom and sits on the bed. She pats the bed with her hand, motioning me to sit down next to her. "Talk to me, Shawn."

"Mom, a few months back, I slept with Amber." I'm looking at her expecting for her to slap the shit out of me.

"Uh huh."

"Mom!"

"Yes, Shawn. I'm listening."

"Well, mom. I told you about the Aaliyah situation. How she basically used me and didn't really love me. Well, at the same time I found that out, Amber found out about one of Khalil's indiscretions. She came over to the house because she needed a shoulder to cry on. I was her shoulder. I've always been her rock, mom."

"Yes, I know."

"Well, one thing led to another, and we made love."

"Well, Shawn, was it good?"

Okay, momz has lost her damn mind. "Mom. What do you mean?"

"I'm just joking with you, baby. Listen, remember mama taught you about Genesis? Genesis means beginning. Its opening verses challenge us to get our priorities right. The priority of God. God comes first, baby. God is greater than our circumstances. Also in that chapter, it says, 'And the LORD God took the man, and put him into the garden of Eden to dress it and to keep it. And the LORD God commanded the man, saying, Of every tree of the garden thou mayest freely eat: But of the tree of the knowledge of good and evil, thou shalt not eat of it.'"

"Yes, mom, I remember."

"Now, you were not to yield to temptation, Shawn. You were Amber's friend and you were supposed to protect and keep her, but not eat from the fruit."

"Mom, I feel so bad."

"But, I'm not surprised, Shawn. You've loved Amber from day one."

"Mom!"

"You did. But you're a respectful man. So you didn't press the issue. Do you remember your aunt Lillian?"

"Yeah."

"Ever wonder why you don't see her anymore?"

"Well, I figured she moved or something, Ma. I was a child."

"And you know that no good father of yours?"

"Yeah, I hate the bastard."

"Well, your father did partake in the forbidden fruit known as your aunt Lillian. Don't follow in your father's footsteps, Shawn."

What my mother just revealed to me made me feel lower than dog shit. But I got her point.

"Pray for forgiveness Shawn. You'll be fine. Now, tell me about this Summer."

My eyes light up.

"Wait, let's go downstairs and eat, sugar."

As we walk down the stairs, I tell momz about Summer and the love I feel for her. "Mom, I mean, Summer is gorgeous. Believe it or not, she looks like Amber a little."

"Oh she one of those light skinned girls?"

I laugh out loud, while admiring the huge plate of collard greens, candied yams, fried chicken, and cornbread. "Yeah, Mom. She is. But she's so much more. She sends me flowers. She has good credit, Ma. She makes me lunch and brings it to me, when she's in the city. She has a good government job. Mom, don't tell nobody, but when we make love, my toes curl."

"Boy!"

"Ma, for real. That's part of the reason I'm down here this weekend. Ma, I want to ask her to marry me. I can't let this one get away. I've made that mistake before."

The tears pour from my mother's eyes, as she pours me a glass of fresh lemonade. "Oh, Shawn." She comes over to hug me around my neck. "Baby, if you love her, ask her 'cause I'm about due for some grandbabies!"

"Speaking of babies, Ma. Amber gave birth to a healthy baby boy last night. I'll go by the hospital when I get home. Khalil was screaming at the top of his lungs when he called. I asked to speak to Amber, but he said she was knocked out."

"I can't believe Khalil is a daddy. I'll send something up there for the baby."

"He asked me to be the godfather. I proudly accepted."

"What's the boy's name?"

"Khalil Shawn Devereaux."

"Wow, that is nice, Shawn. Does Khalil know about you and Amber?"

"No. We decided to let go and let God. I still love her though, Mom, but my life, my world is Summer."

As we get our grub on and toast our lemonade glasses in celebration, the tight sounds of Brian McKnight's *Never Felt this Way About Loving* coming from my cell phone interrupts. My baby is on the line. I wipe my hands and open the flip.

"Hey, sweetie. I miss you already."

"I miss you too, Shawn. When are you coming back?"

"Tomorrow night. And I have a surprise for you."

"What is it?"

"Aw, Summer, you'll have to wait until I get there."

"Shawn! You know I can't handle surprises, baby, please."

"No, sweetie. But I'm sitting here with momz, say hi."

I hand the phone to my mother, and she smiles, clears her throat. "Hi Summer. This is Shawn's mom. I've heard so many nice things about you." She hands the phone back to me, and continues eating.

"Yeah baby. So I'll be back tomorrow after momz and I do Mother's Day dinner, okay?"

"Yes, baby. I love you, Shawn."

"I love you too, Summer."

"Oh, Shawn?"

"Yeah, sugah?"

"Your mom won't be the only one celebrating Mother's Day."

My heart just ascended to my throat. She's got to be talking about Amber.

"Oh yeah. Amber will be too."

"Yeah, Amber too, and…"

"Summer, what are you saying?"

"I'm pregnant, Shawn."

"I love you, Summer! Okay, I'll leave early tomorrow, baby. Oh my God, Summer. Go lay down, baby, get some rest, I'll be there tomorrow. Momz and I will do breakfast, then I'm on the road. Are you okay? Baby, go lay down. Oh shit, I'm losing it. Summer! My baby is going to be having my baby."

"Shawn, I'm fine sweetie. Enjoy the time with your mom, and I'll see you tomorrow."

"Bye, baby."

"Bye, Shawn."

Taking a deep bite into my luscious and moist chicken breast, drenched with hot sauce, my cell rings again. Damn, I really want to fuck this meal up. Summer can cook her ass off, but momz is reigning supreme, hands down. Opening the flip, fingers full of chicken grease, I answer.

"Hello?"

"Hi, Shawn. How are you?"

"I'm fine, Amber. Are you feeling okay?"

"Yes, I'm good Shawn."

A brief and awkward silence greets both of us on the line. This is too strange. "Amber?"

"Shawn, you have a son. Congratulations."

A Word from the Author

Grace & Peace Family,

It is with great respect and sincere heartfelt appreciation that I thank you for reading *Point of No Return*. As many authors will tell you; writing is a passion. And it's true. Writing is my passion and I'm so blessed to be able to share my passion with so many, and you in turn, have been so moved and entertained by my words, and that is one of my greatest joys.

Speaking of being entertained…

Don't you just hate Shayla? I know I can't stand her ass and if you feel anything like me, you want her to catch syphilis, and go straight to hell with gasoline drawers on. How about that Shawn? Mmmm, is all I'll say. Poor Khalil. Do you like Summer? I love a strong black woman, don't you? I hope you enjoyed the sequel to *Good to the Last Drop*, because it was indeed a pleasure to write.

First, let me start off my acknowledgements by saying Happy Birthday to my Daddy! I love my daddy something serious and thank God for blessing me with someone who not only created me, but who is also one of my closest and dearest friends. Happy Birthday Daddy. I love you with all my heart and soul.

I give all the praise to God, from which all blessings flow. My road has been intensely rough, I've traveled many miles, and have many more to travel. Yet, by the grace of God, I've come this far, and wouldn't change nothing for my journey now.

Giving thanks to my husband for sustaining and balancing my life. My children for continuing my life, and bringing an undeniable warmth to my spirit. My parents for giving me life, and nurturing the seed you've created. I am, because of you. My mother for being my peace in the storm.

We can't accomplish much in life without a positive and reinforcing core in place. Therefore, I'd like to take this opportunity to acknowledge and thank some of the people in my life who've been there through triumph and tragedy, yet have remained steadfast in their commitment. Y'all know how people are and how haters do. They always busy, ain't they?

My dearest friends, Paula, Fuquan, Regina, Lawrence and my cousin Shawna. I love you infinitely.

Thanks to my friends, family and literary colleagues; Ruth, Max Julien, Jessica Tilles, Claudia Brown Mosley, Lalaina Knowles, Loretta, April, Stanley, James Lisbon, Kisha Canty and Jimmy D. Your support and encouragement doesn't go unnoticed.

Special thank you and shout out to APOOO Book Club, OOSA Online Book Club, Books 2 Mention magazine, Disilgold Magazine, Big Time Publishing Magazine. I thank you for such a fair and honest review of *Good to the Last Drop* and for supporting me in my literary endeavors.

Are you ready for more? To all my devoted readers; stay tuned for *A Whisper to a Scream* and *The Triumph of My Soul* coming soon. Also, be prepared for the anthology, *Dipped in Black*, coming in 2008.

If you feel like I forgot to mention you, and you sincerely feel like I should have, please feel free to put your name right here
_____. ☺

Love you for reading, I'll Holla.

Elissa Gabrielle
May 31, 2007, 2:13 a.m.

Peace in the Storm Publishing Titles
"Giving Your Soul A Rise...One Page at a Time"

_____ *Good to the Last Drop* by Elissa Gabrielle $16.00
ISBN: 978-0-9790222-0-3 & 0-9790222-0-7
_____ *Point of No Return* by Elissa Gabrielle $16.00
ISBN: 978-0-9790222-1-0 & 0-9790222-1-5

Please include $3.00 shipping/handling for the first book, and $1.00 for each additional book.

Send my book(s) to:

Name:_____
Address:_____
City, State, Zip:_____
Telephone:_____
Email:_____

Would you like to receive emails from Elissa Gabrielle?
____Yes   _____No

Make checks and money orders payable to Elissa Gabrielle.

Peace In The Storm Publishing
Attn: Book Orders
P.O. Box 1152
Pocono Summit, PA 18346

Visit on the web:

www.elissagabrielle.com
www.peaceinthestormpublishing.com
www.GreetingsFromTheSoul.com

Elissa Gabrielle would love to
hear from you!

Contact her at
ElissaGabrielle@yahoo.com

Printed in the United States
141074LV00002B/52/A